A Candlelight
Regency Special

BOLD VENTURE

Colleen Moore

A CANDLELIGHT REGENCY SPECIAL

Published by
Dell Publishing Co., Inc.
1 Dag Hammarskjold Plaza
New York, New York 10017

Dell ® TM 681510, Dell Publishing Co., Inc.

ISBN: 0–440–10517–X

Printed in the United States of America
First printing—December 1981

CHAPTER ONE

"What a dreadful word," Millicent protested.

"Coconspirators? But we are, aren't we?" Sarah replied, the older woman's eyes sparkling with an impishness that belied her years.

"Not at all. You make us sound as though we were common criminals," Millicent retorted indignantly. Sarah's face clouded in a moment of thought.

"Some would say as much," Sarah remarked.

"*Some* will say anything. I couldn't care less about *some*, you know that. I care only about those who are important," Millicent returned as Sarah went on inside with the geraniums she'd fetched. Millicent Hardesty's brown eyes fastened on the great house and she felt the silent words well up inside her. *Haddington Hall was alive again.*

The magnificent, tall, oak front door was waxed and polished, smooth and shining once again, the handmade brass fittings gleaming. The steep-pitched hip roof with the dormer windows had been thoroughly cleaned and the glass of the tall, arched downstairs windows with their hint of bar tracery were now washed to crystal clearness. Inside, maid-servants and butlers once again silently trod the polished parquet floors and in the main drawing room with its trompe l'oeil east wall, the great burnished-gold curtains glistened in richness once more. The great chandeliers of Murano glass were waiting to shower every gilded and carved cornice with light.

They had but a few hours to wait, Millicent Hardesty murmured silently. This very night the great house would blaze with light and once again the elegant carriages would draw up to the door—calèches and Panel-Boot Victorias, broughams, and twelve-quarter coaches—all bringing the elegant and socially important guests. Haddington Hall would resound again to the tinkle of champagne glasses and silver brandy goblets, the laughter of charming women in the latest of fashionable gowns with their proud escorts. Byron had once danced in the main drawing room and Richard Sheridan had taken his whiskey in the study.

Indeed, Haddington Hall lived again as well it should and Millicent Hardesty felt her eyes glisten with an unexpected rush of pride. The great house lived again because she had brought it back to life.

With Sarah's help, she added quickly. Even in her own private thoughts, Millicent was scrupulous about giving credit where credit was due. Without Sarah's help it would have been nigh on impossible. It was more than a dream come true, she thought as she gazed at Haddington Hall from the flagstone terrace, behind her the circular driveway lined with rounded rhododendron bushes, and in the center a marble copy of the famed Farnese Hercules, whose original stands in the Naples Museum. Yes, it was not so much a dream come true as it was a dream made true, fashioned and stitched together as carefully and expertly as the gown she would wear later this night.

Millicent's eye flicked to the nearest tall window as Sarah's ample form appeared with one of the maids carrying the table linen. She felt a tiny smile turn the corners of her lovely lips. The Haddington crest on the napkins had been Sarah's idea, a lion rampant within a double tressure, gules in the first and fourth quarters, argent within. It was the perfect touch for the tables. Sarah disappeared from the window and Millicent's gaze swept over the tall house once again. The lines came to her mind, returning from her schoolgirl drama classes, from Shakespeare, *The Tempest*. She marveled silently at how the mind summons up appropriateness without command, a silent ally.

"There's nothing ill can dwell in such a temple,"

she whispered. "If the ill spirit have so fair a house, good things will strive to dwell with it."

A bit more than passing thoughts, a bit less than a prayer, Millicent thought, and stepped across the flagstones to go into the house. She crossed the spacious foyer, past the drawing room and study, and found herself in the kitchen. The huge open hearth greeted her, its blackened grill wiped clean, a soft bed of glowing embers already under it. She took in the rows of gleaming copper kettles, and the iron skillets, all hanging from ceiling hooks, the wide, tin covering jutting out over the hearth, and the two long cutting tables of sturdy maple.

William Robers, the master chef, was overseeing the tasks of four apprentices brought in for the occasion. He glanced at Millicent as she entered, and nodded deferentially. A long, lean man, he had been retired and an old friend of Sarah's and had allowed himself to be coaxed to take on the kitchen for a fancy price and a promise that there'd be no more than two grand dinners per month. Millicent had been quick to agree, quite aware that one a month was most likely her limit, her budget being definitely exhaustible.

"Is the menu finished, William?" she asked.

"Yes, m'lady," the chef answered, reaching beneath a stack of pans to bring out the hand-lettered *carte*. He gave it to her with both pride and anxiousness in his long face. Millicent's glance went down the list of palatables about which she had briefly conferred with the chef. She gave William Robers a quick, sideways smile of approval, and saw him quietly beam at once.

"Very good," she commented. He had done precisely as she had instructed him, a task of some subtlety for she hadn't wanted a dinner *à la française,* so much the vogue in London now. "Positively everybody's doing that," Sarah had said with her usual peremptoriness.

"A hint of the continent, a gastronomic wink," Millicent had told him, and the *carte* in her hand was testimony of his talents.

Ham and 3 fowls boiled
A chine of mutton with soubise sauce
Fillet of veal with mushrooms
Lark patties with truffles

French plums
4 Brandy-fruits française

A centerpiece of five different ices and around them dried fruits: grapes; apricots; prunellas, greengages.

"Most excellent," she said, handing the menu back to William and moving from the kitchen to the dining hall, her glance sweeping the table already set. She had decided on the ornateness of the *faïence,* the Rouen plates, with the contrasting simplicity of the

11

Chilton flatware. She stood silently for a moment and suddenly her palms were wet with perspiration. Millicent turned away, and started up the delicately curved stairway to find Sarah at the top of the stairs. The older woman stood beside her as she gazed down at the wide sweep of the foyer. Millicent Hardesty drew a deep sigh. Her face, soft-cheeked with a nose that could only be described as pert, took on a look of apprehension. She felt Sarah's hand on her arm, a comforting touch.

"It will go off perfectly, my dear. Don't you fret," Sarah offered. "You've worked too hard for anything else but success."

"I know there are a dozen little things to do yet. I just know it," Millicent bit out.

"I'll tend to them," Sarah assured her. "You go to your room and rest. You'll be the one on your feet all night, the sparkling hostess, Lady Millicent Hardesty. It all rests on your beautiful shoulders, my dear."

Millicent nodded a trifle grimly. Sarah was right, of course. It was up to her to make it succeed. It had been her idea from the very beginning and sometimes she had almost faltered. It had entailed so much more than she'd originally thought about, so many, many more details, each of them important, each a necessary part of the whole. She felt drained, suddenly, and pressed Sarah's hand in a moment of silent gratitude before hurrying to her room.

She halted there before the full-length mirror with

the cupid sitting atop it, unbuttoned the simple afternoon work frock, and let it fall to the floor. She looked at the figure in the mirror, the brown hair tinged with auburn that fell loosely around her face, her shoulders smoothly rounded, her bustline high and firm, her waist small. Lack of beauty had never been one of her problems. If anything, she had too much of it, Millicent reflected, if one can have too much beauty. She'd never used her loveliness consciously, with the guile she'd often seen other beautiful girls use their charms. Until now, she murmured silently, feeling her lips tighten. Now she would use every bit of charm she possessed.

She lay down on the wide, hard-springed bed atop the pale-blue sheets in only her underskirt, stretched her body out, and closed her eyes. She desperately wished to sleep but her mind refused to cooperate, almost maliciously, she thought, turning on her side in annoyance. All that had happened to bring her here seemed to be rushing back at her, from that very first day, everything so absolutely clear. The letter had started it all, of course. That morning when it arrived was indelibly marked in her memory.

CHAPTER TWO

It had been an ordinary morning for Toowoomba, dry as dust with the Australian sun already turning the streets into long griddles on which one could fry an egg. It was Sarah's morning to sleep late and hers to open the shop, and Millicent busied herself blowing the powdery dust from just about everything on the shelves. It was an almost daily necessity.

Australian Artifacts, read the sign over the door. The shop had been Jock's idea, stocked with a melange of items, a helter-skelter array; boomerangs, aborigine masks, spears, carvings, giant conch shells from the Barrier Reef, digger's hats. "Something for everyone," he had said. But when Jock had been killed, suddenly and wrenchingly, trying to prove himself as good with a wild horse as any *ringer,* the shop had become all hers. Three years of moderately happy marriage had ended, all so abruptly, senselessly. It had been Jock's idea to come to Australia from England, a land of opportunity, he had said. But he had found only sudden death.

Millicent felt trapped and realized she was partly to blame for the feeling. The shop could do much better. She just wasn't terribly good at running it, neither as a buyer nor as a seller. Jock had had the knack of it, not her. She'd taken on Sarah as help and had found a firm friend in need, another expatriate from England though in a far different way. Sarah Elkins had come to Australia with a landed family who'd promptly lost everything in a sterile gold mine, leaving her stranded. Since Jock's death, Sarah had helped Millicent through many a lonely night with her stories of all the fine families she had worked for as a nanny and companion back home.

But the feeling of being trapped persisted. It was worse some mornings than others, but Millicent always felt entirely insignificant here, somehow misplaced. It was a country still too full of raw edges for her tastes, an overwhelming place. The feeling was strong on the morning the letter had arrived. Her gaze lingered on the return address of the envelope, engraved in a flowing, Spencerian script:

Robert Ackrood, Barrister
No. 7 Clerkenwell Rd.
London, England

The very address brought a rush of homesickness, even for the London dampness. She opened the letter with one of the horn letter openers for sale atop the counter, and felt the tiny furrow deepen on her brow as she read the neat quill script.

My Dear Madam Hardesty:

It is my regretful duty to inform you that Sir Thomas Haddington, 4th, has of recent date, died in his sleep. As Sir Thomas's barrister for many years, it has been my task to see to his estate.

As you may know, Sir Thomas was a lifelong bachelor and a thorough search of the family records revealed that there are no immediate heirs. Indeed, though you are but a distant niece, you are the only living descendant of the family.

Sir Thomas stipulated in his will that Haddington Hall should be retained in the family and as you are the only "family," I hereby inform you that Haddington Hall is now yours. Sir Thomas passed on leaving no other estate of any value.

I must also inform you that Sir Thomas had not resided at Haddington Hall for the past decade, having been a rather thorough recluse in his latter years. A half-dozen footlockers of small items, silverware, kitchen implements, and his collection of valuable dishware has been in storage at Hinkworth & Sons.

If you wish to dispose of Haddington Hall, I must inform you that the back taxes, plus the inheritance levy and other accountings, will most likely just equal the sale price.

I wait on your word regarding Haddington Hall. At your service,

Respectfully,
Robert Ackrood, Barrister

Millicent felt herself slide onto the straight-backed chair, still staring at the letter. She sat staring at it for a considerable time, letting her thoughts ebb and flow inside her as they would. And flow they did, catching hold of her in most surprising ways. The letter seemed to have set off a veritable host of long-simmering resentments, angers, and frustrations and slowly, out of it all, a single thought gathered itself and skittered about, as if reluctant to take shape, yet refusing to be pushed aside. Millicent was still sitting in the chair, the letter still in her long, sensitive fingers, when Sarah arrived to peer at her in immediate concern.

"You all right, love?" the older woman questioned, swerving her ample shape around the end of the counter.

Millicent focused her attention on Sarah, requiring a moment's determined effort to do so. "All right? Yes, I think so," she murmured.

"You think so?" Sarah pressed.

"Well, it's not every day one gets a white elephant," Millicent answered, thrusting the letter at the other woman. "Here, have a look for yourself."

Sarah took the letter, and read it quickly as Millicent watched, looking up with her brows raised. "You're an heiress, my dear," Sarah remarked.

"Some heiress. You'll pardon me if I don't leap for joy," Millicent flounced. "Or perhaps you'd best read that last paragraph again."

Sarah glanced down at the letter once more and Millicent saw her lips purse. "Yes, I quite see what you mean," the woman murmured.

"It does have the air of a pale pachyderm, agreed?" Millicent said.

Sarah nodded, her round face pressed together for a moment. "I fear so," she said soberly. And then, "But it has livened up your morning. Always look on the bright side, my dear." She handed the letter back as Millicent made a face, "You never told me you were from a titled family," she remarked.

"Sir Thomas was titled. My side of the family were distant relatives," Millicent said with her usual honesty.

Sarah looked thoughtful. "Still there is a title there. I don't quite know where this places you in the social hierarchy of such things."

"It makes me owner of a house I can't possibly

19

afford and will get nothing from when I sell it," Millicent snapped.

"Do you know that place at all?" Sarah queried.

It was Millicent's turn to look thoughtful. "Know Haddington Hall? Yes, in one way only, as a place of wonderful memories. I was very young then, a little, little girl, and quite awed by it. Growing up, I heard talk of Haddington Hall, usually when my side of the family gathered. I remember that we were never invited there except for the holidays. That was apparently a time when all relatives were included in the family spirit, even the least of them. Noblesse oblige, I suppose."

"Then you do have memories of the place," Sarah said.

"Oh, yes, lovely ones, few and far between as they were. But then Uncle Thomas became more and more of a recluse," Millicent said.

"Yes, from the barrister's letter it would seem so. It implies that your distant relative hardly invited anyone there during the time you were growing up," Sarah said.

"Probably not," Millicent thought back. "My memories are those of a little girl. I didn't visit Haddington Hall at all as I grew into a young lady. I do remember talk that no one visited there anymore." She paused, a half-smile touching her face. "But once it was quite the center of social life, a beautiful and splendid place," she added with a sense of wistfulness that surprised her.

"I suppose you'll write Mr. Ackrood to try and find a buyer," Sarah said.

"I suppose so," Millicent replied, saw Sarah's glance turn sharp and her head tilt slightly to one side. Sarah was always quick to catch the unsaid.

"Just what does that mean?" Sarah asked.

"It means I'm really in quite a bother," Millicent flung out. "Actually quite angry, to be truthful about it."

"At what?" Sarah frowned.

"This, blast it," Millicent bit out, waving the letter in one hand. "This inheritance," she said, leaning on the word. "This gift which is no gift at all. The more I thought about it, the angrier I became. It's quite like giving a child a sailboat that can't sail. That's a double-fraud. It's especially hurtful, worse than not having received anything in the first place."

Sarah waited, aware that Millicent hadn't at all finished. "Go on, you've more sticking in you," she said.

"So I have, a good deal more, not all firmed up, mind you, just a rash of thoughts."

"Let's have one," Sarah persisted.

"I've been thinking, what if I just went back and took over Haddington Hall," Millicent tossed out. She saw the older woman's eyebrows lift at once. "I don't mean just go back and sit there until the tax collector carried me off with it. But perhaps this is a sign, a portent." She waved the letter, a little theatrically, she admitted inwardly. "Signs come in many ways, you know," she pronounced.

"So they do," Sarah agreed calmly.

"Look, what do I have here, Sarah? A shop, which I don't really run very well in a place I rather much dislike. I'm a young woman, more than averagely attractive, at a dead end in her life. I should be finding a husband, someone worth what I have to offer as a woman, a wife, an individual. I want to find someone I can love, wholly and completely. But there's nothing here but stockmen and farmers as dry as the land they work all day to earn a grubby living. I won't settle for that."

"Go on," Sarah said.

"I know I can get a good price for the shop. The right person could really make something of it," Millicent said.

"True," Sarah agreed.

"I could get enough to return as the mistress of Haddington Hall. I could go back in high style, for a while, at least," Millicent went on, warming to the thought even more as she put it into words. "How often have you told me that finding a wealthy husband is a matter of moving in the right circles."

"Most usually," Sarah nodded.

"Not that I'd settle for just a wealthy husband," Millicent added quickly, frowning into space for a moment. "But there must be men who are both wealthy and attractive. I'm sure that in all of London high society there is someone I could love."

"Probably, though many of the most attractive ones tend to be cads and bounders, I'm afraid. Wealth and good-looks seem to impart a feeling of crass superiority to men, as though everything else existed for their amusement," Sarah commented.

"I'm sure I can find someone I can love, someone worth loving or, more accurately, have him find me. I intend to move into those right circles, Sarah, to play the role properly, to the hilt, actually," Millicent said, leaning forward impulsively, and taking the older woman's hands in hers. "Don't you see, Sarah, it's my one chance to break out of this dust-ridden cul-de-sac."

Sarah's eyes narrowed, surveying her as if seeing her for the first time. "I didn't realize you had so much of the gambler in you. That's what it would be, you know, a bold gamble, all or nothing."

"Precisely," Millicent snapped back.

Sarah's eyes stayed appraising. "You've beauty enough for it," she said.

"I know I can do it, with your help," Millicent said, growing excited again at the thought.

"My help?" Sarah frowned.

"Yes. You'd come with me, as a companion. A proper lady needs a companion, doesn't she?"

"Unquestionably," Sarah said.

"I need to learn all the things you know, that you can teach me—about proper etiquette, proper manners, how the game is played in those circles. It's different, I know, with its own set of rules. And you know who's who, all the right people to impress. You know how it's all played."

She paused, and watched Sarah's lips purse out, the frown crossing her face, thoughts swimming back of her eyes. "And you want to go back as much as I do," Millicent reminded her. "How many nights have you said that, wished for a way. Well, here it is, waiting for you."

"You're hitting low," Sarah growled.

"Of course," Millicent admitted cheerfully. She waited, her breath held, then saw Sarah's face begin to soften, and curl into a slightly sly smile.

"It might be a jolly good show," the woman allowed and Millicent's arms were around her at once, as far as they could reach, that is.

"It will be all of that, Sarah. We'll enjoy every minute of it, I know. And I'll make it all work, you wait and see," she promised.

Sarah pulled back, and regarded her sternly. "It won't be all beef and gravy, you know," she said. "There's a terrible lot for you to pick up on in not much time. We don't want you coming on as a 'cottage countess,' you know."

"I shan't do that, you can rest assured. Oh, Sarah, this calls for a celebration, champagne, though I just happen to be out of that," Millicent said.

"A glass of lunatic soup, then," Sarah said, using one of the numerous Australian terms for their beer.

"Coming up," Millicent said, turning to the counter and bringing up a pitcher from the bottom shelf, followed with two heavy-bottomed glasses.

"To Lady Millicent Hardesty, mistress of Haddington Hall," Sarah intoned, raising her glass.

"Doesn't that sound perfectly wonderful?" Millicent beamed, taking a long sip of the beer which she had finally grown used to, though not fondly. She raised her glass again.

"And to love," she said, suddenly serious. It would all be for nothing without that.

CHAPTER THREE

That night, Millicent's usual bedtime passed with her lying very wide awake in the bed. Sleep seemed simply impossible, so much so that she rose, went into the kitchen, and fixed herself a pot of jasmine tea. She took the cup of brew into the living room, with only the low lamplight on, and curled herself into the overstuffed chair, wrapping her robe tight against a touch of night chill that permeated the house. She sipped the hot tea, her auburn hair falling loosely around her shoulders. It was suddenly terribly important that she remember everything she could about those childhood visits to Haddington Hall.

Sàrah was going to be her teacher, guide, and mentor, but everything she could recall on her own would have its special importance. That would be the remembering no one could teach, the inner knowing that spoke with its own voice, dim and distant a voice though it might be. She closed her eyes and let her mind float backward, drifting off on a sea of its own. The years began to peel away as if they'd never stood between now and then. Details began to reappear, times she had thought forgotten, moments and moods, times and tempers, sights, sounds, smells, all imprints on the heart.

What part did they play in the decision she had made this day? she wondered. Perhaps more than she realized, more than she would ever know. Had the seeds of the Lady Millicent Hardesty been formed way back then? Had the strength for this bold venture been given her in those distant times? Warmth, happiness, sweet and wonderful moments, they stayed inside the heart. Did they just wait to be reawakened? Did they wait for their opportunity to prod and pull at us, to make us hark back to moments we never wanted to end? Did the warm and happy moments of our childhood never stop beckoning to us, calling us back?

Millicent felt herself returning to another time, a time of childhood awe when almost everything seemed wondrous. The Christmas visit to Haddington Hall had always been the most exciting. Sometimes she seemed to live from Christmas to Christmas for that moment, everything in between only so much meaningless time. She saw it all again, yesterdays coming alive, flooding back over her.

They always arrived at Haddington Hall the day before Christmas and she was given her own room adjoining that of her parents. Uncle Thomas always wore a red velvet smoking jacket with a ruffled white shirt and a high collar. Millicent, of course, was always clothed in her very best visiting outfits, a percale smock with a small tartan fichu for casual moments, a velvet gown, plus bonnet and pantaloons in jaconet muslin for the dress-up moments.

Arriving on the day before Christmas had a double importance. It permitted one to take part in all the Christmas Eve tree-trimming festivities and to be there, in the afternoon, when the yule log was drawn into the house by horse through a side door. The huge log was, of course, put to the fire that evening and burned throughout Christmas day. The yule log was drawn into the house by a gleaming black shire with long furry legs which made it seem as though he wore boots. The placing of the yule log in the great stone fireplace was accompanied by numerous toasts and a strong-smelling brew brought in by a huge, silver bowl. Years later she learned that the brew was, of course, the spice-laden Christmas punch of whiskey and brandy and the silver bowl the traditional wassail bowl.

"A nod to the heathen gods is in order," she remembered Uncle Thomas saying. "Especially as we've adapted so many of their customs for our celebration."

The remainder of the day was spent taking part in

29

watching and, of course, tasting wherever possible, every step in the making of the Christmas puddings and brandy butter, the special eggnog which, because of the holiday, the children were permitted to sample. Cookies of all sizes, shapes, and tastes descended upon the house: gingerbread men, star-shaped butter cookies, marzipan confections in the shape of apples, potatoes, carrots, and a host of other fruits and vegetables and, of course, chocolate truffles flavored with Barbados rum.

Of course, Uncle Thomas had a staff of expert cooks in the kitchen to prepare all the delicacies so avidly feasted upon by everyone, Millicent recalled. On Christmas Eve Uncle Thomas presided over his special interest, the setting of the crèche. Long before it became commonly popular, he had begun collecting the figurines made by Bavarian craftsman, those from Sicily and Genoa, and finally the greatest of crèche figurines from the Neopolitan artists. It was more a work of art than of devotion to him, Millicent realized many years later, but it was still a project of awe and beauty, and she and the other children were permitted to arrange the many different figurines that made up the biblical scene.

Christmas day brought early risings and presents and then the Christmas dinner, the long polished dining table set with a tablecloth of Irish lace, fine bone china, and each goblet and wine glass sparkling with the reflected light from tall white candles. Each candle wore a small holly wreath at its base, Millicent remembered. Uncle Thomas insisted on roast goose for Christmas dinner, most often a brace, flanked with applesauce and mounds of mashed potatoes looking like so many miniature clouds. Cinnamon flavored parsnips were a tradition, and the only time she ever ate parsnips, Millicent recalled. Accompanying savories and relishes were too numerous to remember and the meal seemed to go on forever.

But the day finally ended and it became time to return home. In its own way, Haddington Hall was like one of the Christmas ornaments that, once the holiday was over, was packed away for another year. Millicent opened her eyes and yesterdays vanished. The great house and her distant uncle hardly played a large role in her young life, and as the years moved on, even the holiday visits came to an end. Yet, as the flood of remembering had just proven, it had all left its mark. Imprints on the heart, she murmured to herself again. Had she always secretly yearned to return to the great house, to be a real part of the gracious beauty of Haddington Hall? Had memories locked inside the heart prompted her decisions, inspired the temerity to embark on so daring a scheme?

Millicent shrugged as she rose from the chair. She knew the question would never be answered. But sleep had finally decided to favor her and she went to bed to fall into a deep slumber in moments. The brave new world waited for her.

* * *

Millicent put the shop up for sale the very next morning with the Herbert Farrows Real Estate Service. It was a quick, quite simple, and, she noted with some surprise, entirely painless act. She was still pondering that fact when she returned to the shop and saw Sarah's sharp eyes probing at her.

"Having second thoughts, love?" Sarah asked as Millicent changed into a brown smock she used when in the store.

"No, not the way you mean," Millicent answered.

"You certainly looked reflective when you came in just now," the older woman said.

"I suppose I'm a bit surprised at myself," Millicent replied. "I had expected second thoughts, apprehensions at the very least, but all I had was an overwhelming sense of relief."

"And you're a bit ashamed at that," Sarah finished.

"Yes, I suppose so. I feel slightly traitorous, putting the shop up just like that, sort of unfaithful to all of Jock's dreams," Millicent admitted.

"You can't both look back and do what you want to do," Sarah said severely. "You'll have to discipline yourself in a lot of ways."

Millicent nodded, and shrugged off her reflections. "So be it, then," she said. "No looking back. The next thing is to send a letter off to the Honorable Robert Ackrood."

"Why don't you sit down and draft one and let me see it," Sarah suggested.

Millicent cast a sidelong glance at the older woman. "I'm simply telling him I'm not putting Haddington Hall up for sale. I can't say anything wrong in that," she remarked, suddenly not at all certain.

Sarah's smile was firm. "It's not a matter of saying something wrong, love. It's a matter of saying things the right way. Everything you do is important from here on. You must be Lady Millicent Hardesty at every moment, now."

"All right, a first draft coming up," Millicent said, and watched Sarah nod approvingly. She surveyed Sarah Elkins, her friend and confidant for so long now, in this wild, bleak land. She took in the ample shape, the large, rounded, open face, full jowled and smooth except for the nest of wrinkles around her eyes, the gray hair pulled back in a bun, the sharp, sparkling blue eyes. It had always been a pleasant, sympathetic face and it was still exactly that, but now Millicent could see the discipline that had made Sarah a companion, housekeeper, and nanny to the best families in England. Sarah could be stern and Millicent was grateful for that, aware that she would have to lean on that inner sternness as well as the walking encyclopedia of manners and social amenities that was Sarah. Not that she, herself, was unschooled in matters of deportment, but the aristocracy of high society had its own codes, its own self-imposed rules. The challenge of it caught at her. She had always responded to challenges, Millicent reflected as she sat down at the little table in the back room and began to compose the letter.

She finished quickly enough and went out to where Sarah waited by the hand-carved boomerangs, one of the faster selling artifacts in the shop. "How's this for a start?" Millicent began, reading aloud. "Dear Mr. Ackrood . . . thank you for your kind letter concerning Haddington Hall and the unhappy demise of Sir Thomas. I have decided that I should like to return to Haddington Hall and therefore I do not wish to contemplate any sale of the house and property at this time. I shall be in further touch with you when my plans become more certain."

Millicent's glance flashed to the older woman, and saw the disapproval in Sarah's eyes. Her face had set itself into a frown without a frown. "Entirely too polite, too nice," Sarah commented.

"Too polite? Too nice?" Millicent echoed, her soft-lined face falling into dismay. "I must say I don't understand that at all," she added, gathering resentment.

"It needs to be more peremptory to ring true. Look down your nose when you write," Sarah said. "Add a slight touch of arrogance. It's part of the aristocratic manner. Try again."

Frowning in dismissal, Millicent returned to the back room. It took two more drafts but finally she had one that satisfied Sarah. She penned the final version in a flowing script.

Robert Ackrood, Esquire
No. 7 Clerkenwell Rd.
London, England

Dear Sir:

I have your communication of the 12th of this past month. Please be advised that I have no intention of selling off Haddington Hall. The very thought is presumptuous. I am returning to take charge of restoring Haddington Hall and will contact you further, probably within the month.

Please inform the proper authorities to this effect. I shall expect your cooperation and services in whatever legal documents are necessary in connection with this matter.

Respectfully,
Lady Millicent Hardesty

"Perfect," Sarah said approvingly while Millicent still looked dubious.

"Will I have to be arrogant, Sarah? I detest arrogant people," Millicent asked.

"I didn't say arrogance," Sarah answered reprovingly. "I said a slight touch of arrogance. There is a fine line of distinction. One is bad manners, the other merely a mark of one's social position, a certain inbred conditioning."

"I shall need to practice very hard on that," Millicent sniffed.

"We shall have to practice hard on a great number of things," Sarah said severely.

"Yes, I know," Millicent agreed meekly. "Where shall we start? We must make every minute count."

It was a vow Millicent found entirely unnecessary to give voice as Sarah, fishing down into her voluminous purse of Australian leather, pulled out a sheet of paper. "I've made a schedule. We'll work both days and evenings," the older woman said. "Mondays, French and chitchat. By the way, how is your French, Millicent?"

"Serviceable, at best," Millicent said honestly.

"Then we'll have to improve that. I've some good French study books you can use. A proper lady must speak her French properly. We don't want any Stratford atte Bow French. Besides, it's the thing these days to sprinkle one's conversation with foreign phrases, particularly French." Sarah arranged herself on the stool, and returned to the list. "Now, Tuesdays will be poetry and art; Wednesdays the etiquette of dress; Thursdays social rules and street etiquette; Fridays china and crystal and Saturdays furniture."

"Couldn't you think of anything for Sundays?" Millicent asked with some tartness.

"I could," Sarah said, fastening her with a straight gaze, "but Sunday is a day of rest. I'm not one to violate the sabbath." Millicent nodded, uncertain whether the sharp, blue eyes held a twinkle or not. "Seeing as how it is Monday, we'll start with French," Sarah said. "Be a dear and get a writing pad for yourself."

Millicent rummaged through a drawer, found a large yellowed pad, and settled herself into a chair. "You should know that the French we speak today in proper circles is rather a recent formal language," Sarah began.

"Recent?" Millicent frowned.

"In terms of languages. Originally, French was spoken in two distinct forms, in north France as the *langue d'oïl* and in south France as the *langue d'oc. Francien* was the dialect spoken in Paris and its surroundings. Not until the sixteenth century did *francien* become adopted as the official language of France. It was actually refined in the Royal Courts and salons but it is still only some three hundred years old. However, the French have made it into the language of culture and diplomacy and the rest of the world has gone along with that, for whatever reasons."

"Do I detect a slight touch of English jealousy there, Sarah?" Millicent nudged.

"You might," the older woman snapped. "However, let's not allow that to interfere with our work." Sarah went on at once, concentrating on those phrases most often a part of the social scene in England, and Millicent used up her writing pad before the day ended and had to find another. But a start had been made and after they closed the shop, they continued work during supper at Sarah's little house. "This business of chitchat is quite important, much more so than it sounds. It's a form of conversational ability that distinguishes the well-schooled lady from the ordinary woman. It is the technique of being able to keep a conversation moving about like a shuttlecock. Let's say that you are at an afternoon drawing-room concert beside a gentleman. The program ends and he turns to you and says, 'That last piece was a German lieder. Are you well up on German?' What do you say?"

"No, not really," Millicent replied.

"Incorrect, love. It leaves your companion with no place to go conversationally except to mumble something and excuse himself or to try again with another question and questions are always abrupt gambits, not at all preferred."

"What should I have said?" Millicent queried.

"No, not really, but my cousin, Cynthia, is quite a student of the language. She's been to Germany," Sarah said. "Now, that allows the gentleman numerous conversational options. He can tell you that he's also been to Germany or ask how your cousin liked the country or whether you contemplate going there. He can even go into German literature. The point being that a proper conversationalist never gives out flat replies but always opens the way for an easy exchange. You would be amazed at how grateful people are to you for this ability, especially gentle-men, many being so verbally awkward."

Millicent nodded as she busily made notes. When she went back to her place, she felt exhausted and slept better than she had in many a night. The days took on their own pattern, Sarah being a strict task-master. "I haven't studied so hard since I was twelve," Millicent grumbled one day, but there was affection in the protest. Actually, Millicent found herself intrigued with the world in which so many little things assumed so much importance.

"Yes, manners are more important than morals," Sarah agreed. "How you do something is more im-portant than what you do. Style, more than content, is the thing. Of course, there are limits. One doesn't take up with the coachman, no matter with what style one does it."

"Couldn't we skip furniture?" Millicent asked one Saturday. "I do know about the impact of the Messrs. Hepplewhite, Chippendale, and Sheraton on furniture design."

"Do you, now?" Sarah returned, one eyebrow lift-ing in a silent statement of its own. "Tell me, what is one of the chief characteristics of Mr. Chippen-dale's work?"

"His ball and claw-foot chairs?" Millicent said, screwing up her face.

"True enough, but there's much more than that," Sarah answered. "What about his center-column pie-crust tables?" she asked. Millicent felt her shoulders lift in a helpless shrug. "And his introduction of mahogany as a major wood for furniture design? Of course, he is famous for his use of chinoiserie, incorporating Chinese design into much of what he did. Now, what would you say characterized Hepplewhite's work?"

Again, Millicent shrugged, and offered a tentative answer: "Delicacy?"

"Yes, but that's entirely too broad an answer. A well-schooled lady will be expected to know specifics and details. Hepplewhite loved to use light-colored woods, particularly satinwood and painted ornament to bring color into rooms made somber by massive Jacobean pieces. His chairbacks are noted for an unbroken curve at the top and the arms set back as are those of a Queen Anne chair. Sheraton's style is straight-lined, relying on simple proportions for its beauty of form. In workmanship, Sheraton loved inlay, particularly light-wood parquetry inlaid on dark mahogany. Sheraton is also known for what he termed, with a quiet wit, his harlequin furniture, designs full of surprises, pieces that concealed and were more than met the eye; a table that opened to become a stepladder, a dressing-stand that became a writing desk by pulling out a hidden section."

"All right, I submit gracefully. No skipping furniture," Millicent said, and by the time the long days were finally at an end she could discourse perfectly not only on the masters Sheraton, Chippendale, and Hepplewhite, but also on the other notable cabinet designers, Edwards and Darley, the Halfpennys, Mathias Lock, and Ince and Mayhew.

As the days went on, Millicent began to be grateful that it took a month before the real estate people found a buyer for the shop willing to offer what Millicent felt was the minimum needed for her bold venture. They finally came up with a Hobart Sledge, a happy-faced man with a large family to help him in the shop and who, Millicent felt at once, was certain to make a success of the enterprise. However, it was another two weeks before Mr. Sledge's funds arrived to complete the transaction, and Millicent bent to her studies with renewed effort.

She thoroughly digested the fact that visits were highly ritualized events in aristocratic regency society. But then, so was just about everything, she murmured to herself. There were Visits of Friendship, Visits of Ceremony, Afternoon Tea Visits, Morning Calls, and Visits of Condolence, each circumscribed with its own set of rules. Afternoon tea visits had to be strictly made up of conversational odds and ends, trifles of talk or gossip. At Visits of Ceremony, one never removed hat or gloves, often not even cape. Morning Calls, despite the name, were made during two and four in the afternoon in winter and two and five in summer so they would not intrude on luncheon and end in time for the hostess to prepare herself for dinner. Friendship visits were the most informal of the lot, but only taken with those one had achieved a certain relationship. Condolence visits were not to be over a half-hour at the most, always with somber-hued garments in attire.

By the time Mr. Sledge's funds arrived and the sale was completed, Millicent had reached that point which she'd feared would come, exhaustion and frustration at how much there was still to master. "I'll never remember it all," she cried. "Never, never, never."

"Nonsense," Sarah said sharply, allowing not the faintest shred of sympathy to show in her face or her voice. "You'll master every bit of it. You're doing quite well."

"Hah!" Millicent snorted. "You're just saying that."

"I never just say things," Sarah returned sternly. "Now let us discuss this business about the active verb *to take*. Will you take tea with us? Will you take some mutton? You've heard that used over and over, undoubtedly have used it yourself, right, love?"

"Right," Millicent said, brightening at once, glad at having done something correct.

"Well, don't use it again, ever," Sarah snapped and Millicent felt herself deflate like a punctured balloon. "It's an expression used by the common masses and not considered *comme il faut*. The active verb *to have* should be the only one ever used. Will you have some tea with us? Will you have some mutton? And the terms *beau* and *belle* are really out of favor, even though they are French. Don't ask me why these two words have been singled out for disapprobation, they just have been."

But the time came for packing, finally, the funds from the sale of the shop transferred to the Bank of London. "The voyage will take the better part of ninety days," Sarah observed. "We'll just continue studying during the trip."

"Yes," Millicent said. "I should want that."

Sarah's oval face burst into a sudden smile that brought a frown to Millicent's brow. "What in heavens did I say?" she asked.

"More than you know. Once again, not so much what you said as how you said it," Sarah told her. "It had the ring of authority. It was proof that all we've been doing has had a coming together. All the bits and pieces, all the information, is important of itself, but it wouldn't mean very much at all if it wasn't working inside you, turning you into the Lady Millicent Hardesty."

Millicent felt darkness move into her brown eyes and a sudden stab of fright pushed at her. "I'm glad for that and I'm also unhappy," she said with characteristic honesty. "Sometimes I think I'm becoming the kind of person I've never really much liked and I don't want that."

The older woman's arms went around her. "Don't worry on that score, my dear," Sarah said. "You won't change, not really. It will all sift itself together in time. Besides, you're loveliness deserves an aristocratic manner."

Millicent stepped back from the older woman, and held Sarah's hands, still surprisingly smooth. "Do you think we'll really pull it off? Do you really think so?" she asked. "It's all been your doing. I'd have been lost without you."

"My part will be over soon enough. The real doing will be yours from now on, love," Sarah said.

"Only because Lady Millicent will have a companion who'll be part adviser, strategist, and general field commander," Millicent said.

"I'll enjoy every moment of it as much as you will," Sarah told her. It was but a few days after that passage was booked on a British flag clipper sailing out of Perth. The letter to Barrister Ackrood informing him of estimated arrival dates had already been sent on its way and Sarah had had the delicious idea of purchasing a half-dozen more trunks and filling them with pieces of wood. "We can't have Lady Hardesty and her companion arriving with but two pieces of baggage between them," she'd commented impishly.

The trip itself was blessed by fair winds and good weather and the vessel was run by a civilized master. But Millicent and Sarah had little time to spend with the other passengers. There was too much hard budget work to be done, planning how far their funds would carry, how much could be set aside for the necessities and for the superfluous items. Millicent was gaining a grudging comprehension of how much the wealthy spent to maintain their way of life. In between budget sessions, sudden questions were tossed at her by Sarah, timed to catch her off guard.

"Street etiquette," Sarah snapped one evening as they were about to go to dinner.

"Always speak first to your milliner, butcher, wine merchant, seamstress, any tradespeople you employ. They will not presume to speak first to you and unless you do so you will appear rude and not a proper lady." Millicent rattled off without hesitation.

"Excellent," Sarah beamed. "Quite important, those little things. Tradespeople are quick to talk good and bad about someone."

It was a rare morning when the sea was rough and Millicent clung to the handrail inside their cabin when Sarah shot another question at her. "Who's Robert Southey?"

"A second-rate poet," Millicent snapped.

"How can you say that? He's poet laureate of England," Sarah protested.

"Only because Sir Walter Scott turned it down," Millicent retorted.

Sarah's beam was pure approval. "Perfect," she said happily.

On a star-filled night soon after, the ship's master made his announcement at dinner: "Tomorrow you'll be in England," he said with more than a touch of pride. Millicent felt a rush of emotions sweep over her, more than simply excitement, and knew her face had flushed. Suddenly it was all looming up in front of her, everything close at hand, now, playacting about to turn into reality, ideas into substance. She reached for the glass of after-dinner port in front of her, and lifted it with a suddenly trembling hand to take a long sip of the deep-red liquid. The moment had gone by unnoticed by all except Sarah as they were immersed in their own excited murmurings. Later, the meal over, on the night deck with Sarah, the older woman's voice held gentle understanding tinged with a hint of wry humor.

"Bit of stage fright, is it, love?" Sarah remarked. Millicent nodded solemnly. "You've just got to ignore it," Sarah said. "It's too late to grow scared, now." She patted Millicent's arm. "Get a good night's sleep. Tomorrow will be a busy day for both of us," she said.

"I'll be along in a few minutes," Millicent answered, and Sarah went to the cabin, leaving her alone on the gently rolling deck. Millicent went to the smooth teak rail, her eyes dark with thoughts as she gazed across the blackness of the night sea and up at the jewel-flecked sky above. She felt very small and alone, but her rush of misgivings didn't concern her ability to carry off all that she had planned. Something deeper tugged at her, misgivings of the spirit and the soul, questions of content instead of simply form. Were grand designs of any real value if they were based on the wrong premise? The question hung before her, and refused to be blown aside. Was this bold venture the way to find happiness? Was this the way to find love? *Love!* The word danced inside her. Had she already settled for something less? Her lovely lips tightened into a thin line as she refused the thought. No, she'd not settled for anything, not yet. Bold ventures and bold loves. They could go together. They had to, she told herself.

But she turned from the silent sea filled with inner wonderings.

CHAPTER FOUR

Millicent, Sarah beside her, hung over the rail as the ship sailed past Southend-on-Sea in the morning sun and headed into the river Thames. Hundreds of tall masts and cross spars were like a curtain of fine lace draped over a window, the city of London rising up behind the row upon row of berthed vessels. Millicent felt a stab of sweet pain inside her as the towers of Westminster Abbey rose up before her and her hands tightened on the rail. *This blessed plot, this earth, this realm, this England,* she murmured silently. A quick glance at Sarah's face gave echo to her words.

The vessel nosed its way into a long wharf just past Southwark Bridge and Millicent watched as the crew made the vessel fast and began to unload the passenger's bags and baggage. She had put on the deep-green traveling dress, her last purchase in Australia, a good, serviceable gown that showed off her auburn-tinted hair. Plans for this first day on English soil had been discussed and set weeks ago. She was to take a hackney to Mr. Ackrood's offices while Sarah saw to purchasing a carriage and hiring a driver for the ride to Haddington Hall, preferably a man who'd stay in their employ. After that Sarah would return to the wharf to retrieve their slightly spurious half-dozen trunks.

"I'll be as quick as I can," Sarah said as they disembarked. "I'm certain the Crothers Stables will have something we can purchase at a not exorbitant price, and they always have a handful of decent drivers looking for a good position." Her sharp blue eyes gave a twinkle. "You set the right tone with our good barrister, meanwhile," she added. She stepped back a pace as Millicent reached the wharf, and raised her voice for anyone within earshot to hear. "I'll get your hackney, m'lady," she said, turned and hurried out into the cobbled street. Millicent followed slowly, amazed at how much dignity that round, ample form could suddenly wrap about itself.

The hackney was at the curb waiting as Millicent reached it, Sarah holding the door open. Millicent stepped into the open-topped cab with but a nod to Sarah, sat back, and gave the driver the Clerkenwell Road address. The rehearsals were all done with, now. The play was on the stage and she would have to perform or fail. She cast a glance about for Sarah as the hackney rolled away and found that the woman had already left. Millicent settled back and tried to still the butterflies in her stomach. This was, she imagined, somewhat the way a young grenadier felt facing his first moments of combat. She heard Sarah's words again: *Don't think about what you'll do or say. That will only freeze you up. Everything you've studied will come to you at the right moment.* Millicent sat back in the cab, drew a deep breath, and let her eyes roam across the London streets.

She looked at sights she had all but given up ever seeing again, Fishmonger's Hall, Fleet Street, Guild Hall and, over everything, the great dome of St. Paul's a mark of things unchanged and unchanging, so terribly comforting to the spirit. The footprints of the English-speaking world were on these streets and in these houses, from Good King Alfred to Henry the Eighth to poor George the Fourth, now holding the reins of the monarchy for his dotty papa. Chaucer and Congreve once lived in these venerable houses, as did John Locke and Charles Lamb, to say nothing of William Shakespeare. It was a humbling place, this London, making anyone with a sense of history feel insignificant in it. It was the core of English cultural and political virility and it was good to be back, to draw in the sights and sounds of it, the very air and odors of it.

The cab came to a halt and she shook away aimless musings as she stared at the narrow, dark-wood door with the polished brass number on it, ACKROOD & FORRESTER, BARRISTERS, on an adjoining plaque. She paid the cabbie, turned the doorknob with a gloved hand, and entered a large reception room lined with bound copies of law journals. Large leather-cushioned chairs dotted the spacious room and a slightly stooped man in a black frock coat appeared to greet her with a somewhat apprehensive nod. Ackrood and Forrester obviously hadn't many young women clients, Millicent suspected. She fastened the man with a faintly imperious stare. "Lady Hardesty to see Mr. Ackrood," she said coolly.

The man shuffled off at once, and disappeared into one of two doors opening from the back of the room. He reappeared in moments, leaving the door open. "This way, please," he murmured. Millicent moved past him through the open door and found herself in an oak-paneled office with straight-backed chairs scattered about, a heavy, dark desk taking up most of one end of the room. The man behind it rose as she entered, and came around the desk to greet her. She saw a tall, thin, spidery-looking figure with a face that matched the body. It seemed made up of only vertical lines, a long, thin nose and a long jaw. Even his eyebrows turned down at the ends to conform. His lips seemed the only horizontal line in his face and they were appropriately thin. Pale blue eyes gazed at her, not able to conceal their surprise.

"You didn't receive my letters, Mr. Ackrood?"

Millicent said almost coldly, with what she hoped was proper hauteur.

"Oh, I did indeed, my dear Lady Hardesty," the lawyer said, pulling a straight-backed chair up to the desk for her.

"You seemed surprised at my presence here," Millicent remarked. The role came quite easily, she noted with some surprise of her own.

"No, no, not at all," the lawyer said. "I just somehow expected someone . . . ah . . . a bit older," he finished, stumbling over words.

"Does that disappoint you, Mr. Ackrood?" Millicent slid at him, enjoying her new role.

Mr. Ackrood's long face seemed to grow even longer in discomfort. "Oh, my, no," he stammered. "I might be so bold as to say I did not expect anyone quite so beautiful, either."

"How kind of you," Millicent said smugly and flashed a quick smile that was more than enough to dazzle the long-faced man. She sat down in the chair and looked up at him with businesslike aplomb. "Now, what papers have you readied for me in connection with Haddington Hall?" she asked.

Ackrood hurried around the desk to the other side, sank down in a swivel chair, and pulled out a large manila file folder. He handed it to her. "These are the deeds, statements, the will left by Sir Thomas, land title clearances, plus a number of tax bills as well as outstanding tradesmen's vouchers. Many of these I can hold for a while until you settle into

Haddington Hall," he said. "But I think you should look them over carefully. It shouldn't take more than an hour. You can examine them now, if you wish. I've some references to see to in old law journals."

"Very good," Millicent said, opening the folder. Mr. Ackrood left the room, reminding her of an animated pencil, and she began reading the bundle of papers. Most of them made little sense to her, full of arcane legal phraseology as they were. The tradesmen's vouchers were unhappily the clearest. Sir Thomas had not been terribly prompt at paying bills, she muttered inwardly. Neither would his distant niece, she added. Perhaps it was all to the good that he had established a practice of tardiness. She had just finished reading the last of the papers, a complex bit about the land clearances, when Mr. Ackrood returned to his desk. He brought out a long, very official-looking document with a dark red seal emblazoned at the bottom. He placed it before her on the desk and handed her a quill pen.

"This is legal title to Haddington Hall," he told her. "It is a sworn statement of your relationship to Sir Thomas and your existence as the last member of the family, plus incorporating his instructions regarding the disposition of the house and my attestation to all the other documents bearing on this assumption of title. It merely needs your signature."

Millicent took the pen and signed with a quiet flourish. "Haddington Hall is now all yours, Lady Millicent," the lawyer said, his long face solemn. "Its value and, of course, its responsibilities. As I originally wrote you, I could have had a buyer for the place. In fact, I'm still quite certain I can complete such a transaction if you decide to put the place on the market."

Millicent allowed the lawyer a faintly disdainful gaze. "But I'm not at all interested in that. I made those sentiments clear in my first letter to you, Mr. Ackrood," she said. "I want to restore Haddington Hall to its former state of elegance."

"Yes, of course. I merely felt that to sell would be more . . . shall we say, materially rewarding," the man said.

"There are other things besides material rewards," Millicent said loftily.

"Yes, I suppose so," the lawyer murmured. Robert Ackrood had a long, thin spirit to go with the rest of him, Millicent decided. Her smile was full of patronizing charm, however. She was just about to ask if she could wait in the outer reception room when the elderly assistant appeared with word that Lady Hardesty's carriage had arrived. As she rose to take her leave, Mr. Ackrood handed her two large keys and a rolled parchment document. "I had the place locked, just as a precaution. There are some valuables inside," he said. "This is the property survey and deed which you should have, also. I'll be filing the title of ownership with the proper authorities. I shall be at your service. May Haddington Hall be everything you wish it to be."

"How kind of you," Millicent said, bestowing one last brief smile on the man as she swept from the office with, she felt, magnificently regal flair. She hurried outside to see Sarah's head poking out from inside a carriage, replete with a driver holding two beautifully matched dark bays. The carriage, dark blue with gold trim, was resplendently elegant. "A full clarence," Millicent breathed as she climbed inside. "How did you manage that?"

"All of it a buy, believe me. Part of an estate being settled in a hurry," Sarah said with a touch of smug pride. "I snapped it up. The bays were both recent drum horses in the Queen's Royal Irish Hussars."

Millicent sat back against the satin interior, deep blue in a diamond pattern, and gazed forward through the curved glass front of the carriage. "The driver?" she asked.

"He worked for the man who died. He was happy to take a new position with his carriage. His name's Rupert Bryner," Sarah said.

"I took official title to Haddington Hall," Millicent announced pridefully.

"How was Mr. Ackrood?" Sarah queried.

Millicent made a face. "A bloodless type, typical of the kind of barrister Sir Thomas would choose. But I impressed him, I'm sure."

"Good," Sarah said. "I went to Fleet Street and stopped in at the offices of the *Times*. I left notices with the proper people. No sense in wasting time, I always say."

The clarence rolled out of the London streets and into the greenery that surrounded the city proper. They passed Epson along Old Brompton Road and rolled on through the softly rolling countryside toward Guildford. Large estates loomed up outside the carriage windows, most half-hidden behind manicured hedges and shade trees. When they reached Guildford, the land grew less settled, the houses further between, and the carriage turned into a lane bordered by a growth of blue spruce. The lane opened to become a large green lawn, the driveway circling it, and at the far end, Haddington Hall rose up on a small mound of land.

The carriage drew up before the old house and Millicent got out at once, aware of Sarah stepping close behind her. She stood very still as she gazed up at Haddington Hall. *Pictures in the mind,* she thought silently. *We draw them, unconsciously we draw them, coloring them out of half-memories, expectations, and preconceptions. Reality is never quite the same,* she acknowledged.

The house was darker than she'd expected, with a darker stone façade, darker wood trim, the front taller and the two wings on either side wider. The center part of the house rose up to a steeply pitched hip roof with a tall chimney to one side, three dormer windows facing the front and below, two tall, narrow windows flanking the dark oak door. The house held a quiet, reserved elegance, rather like a grand dowager that had known better times but wore her worn velvet cape with regality.

With Sarah at her side, Millicent turned the large key in the front door, excitement suddenly pulling at her. The door swung open and she entered the stillness of the grand foyer, a wide and spacious area of black-and-white floor tiles in a checked pattern and walls adorned with trompe l'oeil landscapes of sunny gardens and fountains sporting nude nymphets. Beyond the foyer, the grand living room opened, dustsheets over the furniture and the walnut-paneled walls in need of attention. Nonetheless, it was an impressive room and it was quite easy to imagine what beauty polish and shine would bring to it.

Millicent moved toward the left wing of the house, and felt a sharp intake of her breath as she came to the grand ballroom, deep blue with light blue trim on the molded wood corner columns and ceiling. Drapes once sparkling white hung from the tall windows, and once again Millicent envisioned the grand beauty of the room when restored. She turned to Sarah, her brown eyes wide and round.

"I have to make it all work, Sarah," she said. "This magnificent house deserves to live again." She paused for an instant, and heard the silent thought inside her. *Just as I do,* she repeated inwardly.

"We'll do it, love," Sarah echoed. Millicent moved on until, with Sarah, she had gone through the entire house, from great stone kitchen to the servants' quarters. The master bedroom was full of dark furniture and drapes that made her wrinkle her nose. "We'll have it redecorated for you in a matter of days," Sarah said.

"Something very light and airy, pink, lots of pink with gold trim, pink sheets, pink walls, pink chairs," Millicent said. She sat down on the large bed, finding it firm and comfortable. "It'll be such fun, making everything new again," she said.

By the time the day drew to a close, they had opened the carriage house so Rupert could stable the horses and bring his own things into the rooms over the stalls, fixed a room for Sarah on the main floor of the main house, and put fresh sheets on the master bed. They had some tinned fish for dinner and tea they found in the cupboard, along with some biscuits that were still fresh. Before turning in, Millicent investigated the big closed china cupboard that took up almost one wall of the formal dining room in the west wing. Sarah came quickly when Millicent's gasp echoed down the hall. The cupboard was stocked full of delftware, more properly French *faïence.*

"I'd forgotten that Sir Thomas was a great collector of *faïence,*" Millicent breathed, lifting one of the plates from its place behind a wooden protective bar. "These are Rouen plates," Millicent said, turning the dish over in her hands. "From the Moustiere workshops. They were famous for their *en broderie* style. See there, along the edges?"

Sarah surveyed her. "I'm impressed. Where did you learn so much about *faïence?*" Sarah questioned.

"My mother was devoted to *faïence,* though she never could afford the real thing. But she used to discourse on it all the time and collect pictures and catalogs from auctioneers," Millicent answered.

She returned the Rouen plate to its place. It was too late to examine the rest of the cupboard's treasures. She'd devote an afternoon to that, she decided with anticipation, but before she closed the heavy wooden doors she noted the line of crystal glasses and goblets, Irish crystal from Dublin and Waterford, the set of salad and dessert plates from Bavaria. When she went up to the master bedroom to sleep, she found that she was exhausted. Excitement could drain as much as physical labor, she was discovering. She fell asleep quickly in an old nightgown, a small figure in the large bed.

She slept well and burst out of bed when the new morning sun came through the latticed window. Outside, the lawn grass was a vibrant green and she hurried downstairs in her robe to find breakfast waiting and a note on the table in the breakfast alcove.

M'lady—Have taken Rupert and the carriage to the city as per your wishes.

Obediently,
Sarah

Millicent laughed softly. Not as per her wishes, of course, but as per the carefully arranged plans. Sarah

60

would spend the day interviewing the necessary servants to bring back for her approval, plus hiring a crew of temporary workmen to help bring the shine and luster back to Haddington Hall. Millicent poured the breakfast tea, and found warm scones in the oven which Sarah had somehow miraculously found a way to bake. She savored breakfast slowly, in a proper lady-of-the-house manner. *Play the role at all times, even when you're alone,* she remembered Sarah counseling. When she finished, she went upstairs, piled her hair carelessly on top of her head, and donned the old, dull-brown smock she used to wear when dusting the store. It was perfect for a lone walk to inspect the ends and lines of the property and generally snoop about. She undid the parchment property deed Mr. Ackrood had given her, spread it out across the bed, and studied it for a few moments, making mental notes of natural markings referred to in the document.

Rolling up the parchment once more, she went downstairs and out onto the lawn, and found the row of hedges that ran from the side of the carriage house. Hands thrust into the front flap pockets of the brown smock, she strolled along the hedges until they came to an end. Her gaze swept the land and spied the thick column of poplars that began a row a few hundred feet beyond, the second of the landmarks she had noted on the document. She walked into the trees, through the sun-dappled darkness in their midst, and emerged on the other side. Bright sun swept down on her at once and she squinted. She saw that the land had suddenly become rougher, and soon found a small stream bordering a dense stand of oaks. The stream marked the north border of the Haddington Hall lands. Her lands now, she thought with a surge of pride. If the bold venture succeeded, she reminded herself at once, she could turn an interlude into a lifetime.

She started toward the stream, sunlight glinting from the shallow waters of it, when she spied the gray stallion on her side of the stream a dozen yards to the left. As she watched, a man appeared by the stallion, knelt on the ground with a tape measure, and measured off a length of the stream's bank. Feeling a frown pushing across her brow, she started toward the heavy stallion. The man, his back toward her when he rose, mounted the horse in one easy motion and turned the stallion toward her. He reined the horse in as he saw her standing there. Millicent's eyes stayed riveted on the man's face, a countenance more than simply handsome, though it was certainly that. He had jet black hair that fell casually across a broad forehead, a straight nose in the center of a face she could only think of as chiseled, all strong planes and angles, and black eyebrows arching over burning blue eyes. The face made her think of a statue of a Roman warrior she had once seen in the British Museum, a somewhat imperious mien to its striking handsomeness.

The man let the horse step closer, halt, and the

burning blue eyes peered down at her. The tape measure, folded now, lay in his left hand. "You are on Haddington Hall land, I believe, sir," Millicent said, suddenly irritated by the waiting in his eyes, as though he expected her to speak first.

"So I am," the man said, a cool amusement in the deep, mellifluous voice. His eyes, she saw, moved down the brown smock she wore, and traveled up to her face, up to the auburn-tinted hair piled carelessly atop her head. Then they returned to linger for another moment on the swell of her breasts, which even the dull outfit couldn't hide. "And who might you be, my little lass?" the handsome stranger asked.

The sardonic, cool amusement was in his voice, in the handsomeness of his face, in a slight curve of his wide, firm mouth. Millicent held the reply that had leaped to her lips, seeing that he obviously took her to be some form of servant girl. She let her eyes drop down demurely for a moment, actually a quick move to avoid his seeing the moment of irritation in them. "I'm in Lady Hardesty's service," she said, bringing her gaze back to him.

"And a bit bold, too, I'd say," the man remarked.

His patronizing tone grated, and Millicent lifted her head to level her gaze at the chiseled face. "Since when is it a bit bold to look to your lady's interest, sir?" she answered.

The slightly sardonic smile that slid across his face did nothing to make him less handsome—or less irritating. He let his lips purse as he examined her again. "Bold," he said slowly. "I'll stand on that." He swung down from the gray stallion and Millicent saw that he was tall, over six feet, his shoulders wide, his figure in riding trousers and white silk shirt open at the neck, trim and muscular. "What's your name, girl?" he asked brusquely.

Millicent pulled a name from the air. "Audrey," she said, not looking away from his brilliant blue orbs. "I should like to tell Lady Millicent who was riding her land, sir," she added evenly.

The firm mouth found a wry little smile. "Of course. Tell her Dean Fowler, her neighbor, was riding her land," he said.

Dean Fowler. Millicent turned the name over inside her. It had the same crisp, arrogant ring to it he had, she decided. Or perhaps it was only the way he had tossed it at her, almost as a challenge. "With a tape measure," Millicent remarked.

Dean Fowler uttered a short laugh that held an edge of harshness. "Indeed with a tape measure," he agreed. "You can't plan without measuring."

Millicent kept her face expressionless. "I shall tell her, sir," she said, and started to turn away. His hand caught at her arm, a firm touch, a touch that was used to being obeyed.

"Just a moment, Audrey," Dean Fowler said. "Tell me something about your mistress. Is she fair-minded?"

Millicent knew she failed to keep the resentment

from flashing in her eyes. "Indeed she is," she snapped.

"The kind who knows the meaning of promises and obligations?" the handsome man pressed.

"I'd say so, sir," Millicent returned.

"Is she pleasant of disposition?" he asked, and Millicent felt her annoyance becoming anger.

"Most pleasant, unless she's given good reason not to be," Millicent sniffed.

His smile was quick, a bright flash in his dark, chiseled face and he threw his head back in a brief, deep laugh. "A fast answer, that," he said, returning his eyes to her. His hand came out to take her chin between thumb and forefinger. "You've plenty of fire in you, Audrey. I like spirit in women and horses. sign of good breeding somewhere in the background."

"Am I supposed to curtsy, sir?" Millicent asked crisply.

He smiled again, and took his hand from her chin. "Maybe you'd like to work for me, Audrey," Dean Fowler said. Millicent knew her lips parted in astonishment and he laughed again. "No need to be so shocked about it, my dear girl," he said. Suddenly his face grew tight, almost hard, the muscles along the line of his jaw throbbing. "If you're itching to run back to your Lady Millicent with a tale, you can tell her not to plan to settle in at Haddington Hall," he bit out.

He spun on his heel, pulled himself into the saddle,

and wheeled the horse around. He paused to look down at her again, the blue eyes roving piercingly across her face. "You could be an unusually attractive little piece with a bit of work," he observed.

Millicent felt herself wanting to fling a barbed answer into his condescending arrogance, but she forced herself to hold her tongue. To do so would be out of character and destroy the role she'd assumed. Dean Fowler continued to gaze down at her, waiting. She returned his waiting gaze with eyebrows lifted. "When a lady is given a compliment, she says thank you," he remarked. "Proper manners, you know."

"I suppose I didn't recognize it as such," Millicent answered. "Not being used to gentlemen's ways."

He gave her a narrow stare that plainly said he had caught the sarcasm in her reply. He laughed suddenly, wheeled the gray stallion around, and galloped away. Millicent watched him until he vanished through the oaks, turning only when he was out of sight. A long breath escaped her and she realized she was quietly seething. Dean Fowler was as arrogant as he was handsome. She felt sorry for servant girls if they were subjected to that kind of presumptious behavior. But his other remarks whirled inside her as she made her way back to Haddington Hall. What had he meant by telling Lady Millicent not to settle in at Haddington Hall? It had the air of a threat, something certainly ominous at the very least. And the tape measure he was using on the stream bank, his words about planning. *Quite disturbing,* she murmured, feeling the frown stay on her smooth brow. Dean Fowler was disturbing, quite the handsomest man she had ever seen. Strength lay in that handsomeness, the imperiousness of the superior.

But his cryptic remarks stayed, newfound companions of an unwelcome nature. She set them aside as she reached the manor house and busied herself with the contents of the big china cupboard. When Sarah arrived back, she had the servants she'd chosen for Millicent's approval: a butler, a downstairs maid, and a chambermaid. Her approval, Millicent realized, was merely a formality, a matter of appearances, for servants were the foremost of backstairs gossips and a lady's companion giving final approval to their hire would certainly cause talk. The butler, Howell, seemed a gentle, elderly man and Millicent nodded her approval at once. The downstairs maid, a sharp-nosed woman of middle years named Agnes Cowlie, offered excellent references. The chambermaid, Miriam Hoddge, young and pretty with a somewhat pouty mouth, seemed to have little to recommend her except eagerness. However Millicent hired her along with the others, of course, aware that Sarah wouldn't have fetched them all out if she hadn't decided they were the best available.

But Sarah, always quick, had caught the moment of hesitation with the chambermaid and later, during a moment alone, whispered a fast aside. "Chambermaids are difficult to come by these days, it seems. Not enough young girls going into the profession,

67

though I don't understand why not. It's a perfectly honorable profession," Sarah told her.

Millicent certainly had no answer and held back telling anything about her own exciting morning until the new servants had been shown their quarters and she and Sarah had sat down to a dinner only a little less primitive than the one the night before. Even then, Sarah surprised her again. "Out with it, my dear," the older woman said, a twinkle of amusement in her sharp eyes.

Millicent couldn't avoid looking crestfallen. "How did you know I'd something to tell you?" she asked.

"You've been fairly brimming over with something ever since I returned," Sarah laughed.

"You just know me too well," Millicent protested, laughingly. "But you are right. There is something. I met the handsomest man this morning. And the most arrogant. And the most disturbing."

"I take it you're referring to one man, not three," Sarah commented.

"Yes, exactly. One man," Millicent replied. "A most unusual man." Quickly, she recounted the events of the morning, the unexpected meeting with Dean Fowler and his strange and cryptic remarks. When she finished, Sarah sat back in her chair, her eyes narrowed in thought. "What do you make of it all?" Millicent asked.

"Not a great deal, I'm afraid," Sarah said. "The remark about Lady Millicent not settling into Haddington Hall is certainly disturbing. Obviously, he was making pointed allusions to something."

"Indeed, but to what?" Millicent said. "I've been wracking my mind about it all day."

Sarah shrugged helplessly. "I'm quite certain we'll find out in time," she said. "But I have the feeling we'd best not wait for that. I think we'd best find out a few things about this striking neighbor of yours. The name doesn't mean anything at all to me."

"How can we do that?" Millicent asked.

"That's simple enough. I'll do it tomorrow. I must go into that little town, Roxbury, for household supplies. They've a nice provisions shop, I noticed. A few casual questions to tradespeople can bring a wealth of information. I daresay when I return, we shall know a good bit about this Mr. Dean Fowler."

"I shan't go with you, then?" Millicent asked, eager to hear things first-hand about the handsome neighbor.

"No, you'll have quite enough to do here. The extra workmen I hired to set the house right will be here tomorrow. You'll have to be on hand to put them to their tasks," Sarah said.

"Yes, that's true," Millicent agreed.

"There's one more thing. Your handsome neighbor might well come calling, from the things he said," Sarah put forth.

"Yes, he might," Millicent said, a flash of anticipation touching her face.

"Don't see him," Sarah said, dashing cold water

on the moment. "Lady Millicent will be indisposed, resting or simply out. You'd best avoid him until we find out more about him and his strange remarks and attitudes."

Millicent met Sarah's stern gaze and knew the older woman was right. There were too many questions about Dean Fowler. It would be foolish to jeopordize all that had been so carefully planned. She answered with a small sigh. "All right, he shall be turned away if he comes calling," she said.

Sarah's smile was firm. "I don't say the man's no good, mind you, but do remember that most bounders and cads are attractive. Part of their stock-in-trade is charm," she allowed.

"You're so consoling," Millicent snapped back. Sarah let her smile grow broader.

"Now let me tell you what I discovered today," Sarah said. "Four of the most important social arbiters live within a few miles of you. The Upsham sisters, whom I speak of as a single entity. They are in London proper, but Victoria Dennison is in Bracknell, Lady Salisbury is in Redgate, and, the most important of all, the Countess de Berrie is in Windsor. Of course, they all have their London town houses or apartments."

"The Countess de Berrie is a real Countess, I presume," Millicent remarked.

"By marriage. She's English by birth. Married the Count de Berrie in Paris many years ago. He passed away soon after the marriage, very conveniently for her, it turned out."

"What a ghastly thing to say, Sarah," Millicent protested.

"Perhaps, but true, nonetheless. It allowed her free rein to indulge in all her personal amusements, all the money needed to do whatever she wanted, and enabled her to become the *Grand Dame* of high society on two continents. Those the Countess de Berrie disfavors are never quite accepted in the inner circles. Those she accepts are accepted by everyone else."

"Sounds terribly dictatorial and arbitrary. A bit foolish, too," Millicent remarked.

"Oh, it's all of those things, but that is the way the game is played in these circles, my dear, and how you must play it for now," Sarah told her. "At least it's only an avenue for you, Millicent, not a goal or a way of life."

Millicent nodded, suddenly feeling grave and very tired. "I shall turn in, I think," she murmured.

"Are you suddenly sorry you embarked on this adventure?" Sarah questioned.

"No, but it all seems so hollow the way you describe it," Millicent answered.

"Hollow people make it a hollow game. You'll make it something more," Sarah said. Millicent hugged the ample figure and hurried up the wide, carpeted stairs to the large bedroom at the head of the second floor. She undressed quickly, put on a new

71

peignoir, pale salmon, climbed into the bed, and let the darkness embrace her. But sleep proved elusive. She found her thoughts straying back to a chiseled head with burning blue eyes and a deep laugh that exploded with sudden heartiness.

Sarah's words swirled at her. Dean Fowler was no cad or bounder, not in the usual meaning of those terms. There was too much strength in that face. He might be hard, thoroughly unpleasant, perhaps even unscrupulous. But they would be the faults of strength, not of weakness. But she pushed that thought aside quickly. There was far too much warmth in his quick smile for evil. She let her musings wander, taking her into idle bypaths of the heart. Perhaps, she pondered, perhaps she had already found the very thing she had come here to find. Perhaps the bold venture had already been won. The thought curled itself warmly around her, like a comforting shawl. Obviously Dean Fowler was a man of means, and even more obviously a man of striking attractiveness. That kind of good looks deserved a dollop of arrogance. She found herself wondering what those strong, well-formed lips would feel like on hers.

Millicent smiled in the dark. She felt deliciously sinful, clasping her thoughts to herself in the darkness. It was a new experience for her, this fantasizing about handsome lovers. She'd never really done it before. Because she had never really loved before, she reflected. A wry sound escaped her as she thought about it. There was something shameful about that unhappy truth, a woman married and widowed and able to say she had not ever loved before. A small tragedy of the soul, perhaps, yet how many were there like her, she wondered. How many young women married, raised families, wore all the robes of respectability and virtue and all without love? They lived full lives that were really not full at all. Marriage implied love. By its very existence it put on the face of love. Yet how often was the main ingredient missing, the heart of what marriage should be never a part of the union?

Too often, she wagered, far too often. For in this enlightened society of England, that repository of freedom, home of fine-sounding speeches and great documents on the spirit of free man and free choice, a strange chasm existed in the social fabric. When the role of women as individuals, as equal inheritors of freedom's rights, came into issue, the portentous documents and fine-sounding speeches became so much hollow rhetoric. Marriages were still arranged for young girls, often with the impunity of an Arab sultan ordering a wife. Of course, the arrangements covered a great spectrum of reasons—marriage as an economic advantage, a settlement of obligations, a step up on the social ladder for family as well as daughter, and last but certainly not least, the demands for marriage society placed on a young woman.

Her marriage to Jock hadn't been arranged in the

manner so many marriages were, yet as she looked back with the unvarnished honesty of hindsight, it had certainly been the result of expectations, other people's expectations. Perhaps a more subtle form of arrangement, she mused, yet no less demanding. She and Jock had grown up together in Tower Hamlets, just east of Billingsgate Market. Her father and Jock's dad both worked on the London docks. From the time they were youngsters, she and Jock found themselves paired off at every family function, at every neighborhood social. The practice continued as they grew older. As a young girl, it seemed expected that she be with Jock, and she could recall all the comments that were a small litany of subtle conditioning.

"Jock and Millicent look so well together."
"They'll make a fine couple one day."
"A girl should be married early."
"They go together like rashers and eggs."
"Why wouldn't they marry one day?"

Made so often and for so long, the phrases became almost gospel. Families were anxious to see a daughter married, their obligations turned over to someone else. Practical considerations, worldly concerns, that was the guiding force. How unfair and how wrong, she knew now, no less so because it had been done without malice or gain, as was the case with many marriages. But it was an arrangement nonetheless, merely a subtler variety. She recalled her mother's words just a few days before the wedding. *You and Jock were meant for each other, my dear, ever since you were children.*

But I don't know if I love Jock, Millicent remembered almost saying but quickly biting back the words. The mention of the word love seemed almost gratuitous, an intrusion into events quite perfect of themselves. Besides, she asked herself, what did she know about that mysterious word? Of course, she had read novels of wild and romantic love. But perhaps they were only the imagination let loose of anxious authors. Perhaps in reality love was what she felt for Jock, a certain comfortableness, a tenderness, a friendship. Everyone and everything assured her that she loved Jock. Even he seemed to accept the fact. But the wondering persisted deep down inside her, inner murmurings of the heart.

So they were married and in the years that followed she had come to realize that she and Jock had been friends rather than lovers. It had seemed enough for Jock, and she had felt disloyal in her secret questionings. Disloyalty and a quiet simmering anger she kept well hidden. No one had ever asked her what she felt or what she wanted. She was not alone in that, she came to realize as the years passed. Arrangements wore many faces.

She had been perhaps more fortunate than some young women, she realized. Jock was a good man, kind, and there were satisfying aspects of their marriage. But there'd not been any wings to it, not ever. That was a dimension she had dutifully closed away, only to realize that there are yearnings one can never close away. While reading Byron one afternoon the full realization had come to her, the poet's words reaching to the very heart of her in one line: *L'Amitié est l'Amour sans Ailes,* Friendship is Love without his wings.

Millicent's thoughts leaped back to the present. Now, after too long, she was touching that truth, feeling the wild wind of those wings. She thought about Dean Fowler and knew that any relationship with that strong man would have wings. Turbulence, also, she wagered, and perhaps pain. But wings, those wings that made love what it was. Millicent turned on her side, finally letting sleep still her musings, and the strong, handsome face of Dean Fowler slowly drifted away.

CHAPTER FIVE

Morning saw the wagonload of workmen arrive soon after Sarah had left for Roxbury with Rupert. Millicent, a list of tasks to be done in hand, assigned one team to waxing and polishing the walnut-paneled walls, another to moving the heavy pieces she was going to replace from her bedrooms to the cellar, a trio to the task of cleaning the tall windows, and a fourth team to polishing the stairways. As the morning progressed, she was quite surprised to see how much was accomplished by the hardworking laborers as she checked on each group during the day.

She sat at the writing desk in the study and began to draw up a list of things that would be needed for the great ball, suddenly not at all that far away. The house was coming into sparkling shape much more quickly than she had imagined possible and she proceeded with the preliminary list on the assumption that the next phase of the plan would proceed on schedule. It was not too early to begin planning the grand ball, Lady Millicent Hardesty's formal move into the social swirl. She had almost finished the initial list to go over with Sarah when one of the workmen came to call her attention to a crack in the lintel under the living room fireplace mantel.

"Leave it," she said. "It's probably been that way for decades." She turned to return to the study, glanced out the window as she did, and froze on the spot. Outside, a heavy-legged gray stallion and rider were moving across the lawn toward the front door, the rider sitting very straight, his jet-black hair falling carelessly over his strong face. No open-necked shirt this time, she saw, but a proper houndstooth jacket and a cravat.

Millicent whirled, and called out for Agnes Cowlie, who came running at once. "A gentleman will be at the door in a moment," she told the maid. "I'm not in to him. Tell him that I've gone out." She paused, and motioned to the maid as the woman started to turn away. "No, not that," Millicent corrected hastily, her mind racing. Dean Fowler might just decide to wait around for her to return, she pondered. "Tell him I'm at rest and not seeing anyone today," she told Agnes.

"Yes, ma'm," the maid said. Millicent lifted her skirt and raced up the stairway past the men polishing the balustrade. Inside the big bedroom, she ran to the window, which looked down on the front of the house and across the broad expanse of the lawn. Keeping herself flattened against the wall to one side of the window in case those piercing blue eyes should glance upward, she saw Agnes open the front door of the house as Dean Fowler pulled on the bell cord. She could see the maid's lips moving and Dean Fowler, legs apart, making some form of reply. Agnes said something else and shook her head, but the man didn't move. Agnes made a final comment and Dean Fowler finally turned away. She could see the tight line of his jaw as he swung back onto the stallion.

As he wheeled the horse around, his eyes swept up to the top windows, surveying the house. Millicent stepped back further against the wall, then leaned forward as she heard the horse's hooves moving away. Dean Fowler rode only halfway down the driveway, halted, and half-turned in the saddle, his eyes surveying the house again, roaming across the lawn and the carriage house. He moved closer to the stables and she could see his eyes narrowed in thought. He turned the horse again, and rode to the other side of the driveway. *He glanced about as though he were inspecting the place,* Millicent thought. *As though it were his to survey.* She felt resentment spiraling inside her. *Perhaps Mr. Dean Fowler looked at everything as though it were his. He had certainly regarded "Audrey" with a proprietory eye,* she recalled.

She watched as he finally rode the gray stallion down the driveway and out of sight amid the spruces. She was still frowning in thought as she went back downstairs. Dean Fowler, for all his striking looks, had a terribly strange way about him, she decided. Agnes was in the foyer as she came down the stairs. "Thank you, Agnes," Millicent said. "What did he have to say?"

"He didn't seem to want to take no for an answer, ma'm," the maid said, and then, after a moment's pause, "I suppose he's not used to it, with his looks and all."

Millicent smiled. *It was an unsophisticated but probably thoroughly accurate observation,* she agreed silently and returned to the writing desk until she heard the sound of the carriage drawing up outside. Sarah bustled in moments later, Rupert following along, pulling a small cart of groceries and green goods. "He was here, only a short while ago," Millicent burst out. "You were right. He did come calling. I had Agnes send him away."

"Good," Sarah said. "I did find out a bit about Mr. Dean Fowler, though. He does own the land adjoining yours, Brandywin Farms, he calls it and he's apparently quite well off. He's from York, bought the place next to yours some ten years ago. I'm told he's heavily into the breeding of a new strain of horses he's trying to develop."

Millicent couldn't hide her smile. "Then he is a man of substance and standing," she said aloud.

80

"He's also quite a rake with the ladies, I'm told," Sarah said.

"That's to be expected, given his looks," Millicent said.

"Of course, none of this explains those strange remarks," Sarah reminded her.

"No, it doesn't," Millicent had to agree. "It's perhaps just his way," she added and caught Sarah's skeptical stare. "All right, it is a strange way he has of riding Haddington Hall land as though it were his," Millicent admitted. "But what you've found out thus far is all positive."

"I've not found out terribly much. I asked and listened to talk. It doesn't satisfy me. Appearances can be created, can't they?" Sarah said, leaning meaningfully on the words.

Millicent's nod carried rueful admission. "Yes, so they can," she murmured. "As we quite thoroughly know."

"Then I suggest you continue to stay away from Mr. Dean Fowler until I've a chance to inquire further about the gentleman," Sarah said severely. Then, gentling her voice at Millicent's crestfallen expression, she added "You'll have plenty of chances to set your cap for him if that's what you're thinking about."

Millicent nodded again. "You're right as usual," she said, not adding that she was feeling terribly curious and full of a schoolgirl's eagerness about

Dean Fowler, a combination not calculated to lend itself to sage and sober behavior.

"Now I've something to show you," Sarah announced, reaching into the large shopping basket. She pulled forth a copy of the London *Times,* and held it aloft triumphantly, her eyes sparkling. "Page eleven," she said, handing it to Millicent. Millicent opened the newspaper and saw that the page was headed *Social Events.* Her eyes went to the little item Sarah had marked with pencil and she read quickly:

> Lady Millicent Hardesty is in residence at Haddington Hall, Guildford.

She lowered the paper, and glanced up at Sarah. "That's it?" she asked. "I had expected something more."

"Such as?"

"I don't know, really. Perhaps something about the ball to formally celebrate my taking over Haddington Hall," Millicent replied.

Sarah shook her head vigorously. "No, no. That would be pretentious. It would smack of trying to push your way into acceptance. Curiosity is the prime moving force. They'll want to meet you, see you and, we hope, accept you. This announcement will enable them to make their first move. It is the piece of cheese set out to bring the mice."

"I see," Millicent said and marveled again at the subtle intricacies of this world of manners and styles.

She returned to her list while Sarah bustled off to the kitchen. She felt good. The information Sarah had learned about Dean Fowler was most encouraging, despite Sarah's stubborn caution. There would no doubt be some perfectly rational and reasonable explanation for his cryptic remarks.

In the days that followed, a pattern quickly established itself: Sarah going into town for supplies and errands, she overseeing the workmen each day as the great house began to glow, the servants settling down to their routines. Sarah had convinced William Robers to take on the kitchen, under his strict terms, and once again Millicent found herself surprised at how wonderfully Haddington Hall was regaining all its former glory. Physically, at least. But a house, just as people, needs qualities of the spirit as well as of the body. Though there were many pieces yet to be put into place in the great plan, she found herself looking forward to the ball with more and more eagerness and less and less trepidation. Lady Millicent Hardesty was beginning to feel quite invincible.

The days grew warmer and it was on a sunlight afternoon, Sarah in town, that Millicent decided to do some gardening, a love she hated turning over to gardeners. Besides, they hadn't hired one yet, an expense she was glad to eliminate. She'd noted that the main hedges needed trimming and she donned the brown smock again, the outfit she had come to call her "Audrey" dress, piled her hair carelessly atop her head, and set out to her task with a basket of gardener's tools she had found in the carriage house. She had snipped along more than half the length of the twin rows of hedges that extended from the side of the house, also turning the ground over at the root line, when she halted, a frown on her brow. Through the hedges, she saw the gray stallion moving slowly across the field. Dean Fowler was sitting very straight atop the horse, dressed in tan trousers and a deep-brown shirt opened at the neck. He moved the horse in a straight line across the field, then turned to form another line at right angles, measuring off a square with deliberate steps.

Millicent pushed her way through the hedge and into the open on the other side, feeling irritation pulling at her. The man saw her emerge from the hedge, and turned the horse to where she had halted.

"Well, we meet again, Miss Audrey," he said calmly, black hair tumbling carelessly almost over one eye. "I only wish your mistress were as easy to come face-to-face with as you."

His eyes roamed over her again, private amusement in them, as though he were making a mental comparision with the first time he had examined her. In fact, she was certain he was doing exactly that, and her eyes narrowed a fraction. "Lady Hardesty did give me a message in the event I happened upon you again on Haddington Hall land," she said.

His eyebrows lifted. "Indeed? Well, that's something, at least. Let's have it, lass."

"I fear it will not be to your pleasure, sir," she said.

"Go on with it, Audrey," he ordered sharply.

Millicent let a smile, a too sweet one, accompany her words. "A gentleman does not ride casually over someone else's lands unless given permission to do so," she said.

Dean Fowler stared down at her and she saw the blue eyes turn into cold crystal for a moment, and stay riveted on her. "Tell your lady that I need no lessons from her," he said after a moment.

"Yet you continue to do so, sir," Millicent returned evenly.

Dean Fowler's eyebrows lifted again and a slow smile touched the edges of his mouth. "I see where you get your boldness from, lass. Your mistress's influence, obviously," he said.

"I told you it would not be to your pleasure, sir," Millicent said.

Dean Fowler's face tightened again. "Tell your lady that I am well aware of both courtesy and of rights," he said sharply.

Millicent studied the handsome face but it told her nothing except that he knew the edge of anger. Once again his remark was wreathed in the unsaid, and full of cryptic meanings. She wanted to demand clarification but held her tongue. There was only so far a servant girl would dare press, even a bold one, she smiled inwardly. "I shall tell her that, sir," she said blandly.

Dean Fowler's eyes stayed hard. "Also tell her that I am forced to wonder if she is avoiding me, though I can understand her doing that well enough," he added. Another remark full of hidden barbs, Millicent noted, and kept the frown from her face with effort.

"I shall add that to the message," she replied.

He leaned down from the saddle with a suddenness that took her by surprise, and cupped her chin in one hand with a firm yet gentle grip. A smile just touched the edges of his lips. "And you could still be an uncommonly pretty little piece with a bit of fixing, even with your nose all smudged with dirt," he said.

Automatically, Millicent's hand flew to her face and Dean Fowler straightened up, his laugh lingering as he galloped off with not another glance or word. Millicent rubbed her nose, looked at her hands full of rich, black soil, and knew she'd only made the smudge worse. Dean Fowler had disappeared onto his own land and she returned to her task at the hedges. He was indeed addicted to veiled remarks, she pondered as her trimming shears flew along the tops of the bushes. Perhaps Mr. Dean Fowler simply needed a lesson in civility and proper behavior. She'd often heard that bachelors were wont to develop perfectly horrible social habits.

She continued to work until the afternoon shadows grew long, finished the last of the hedges, and returned to the house to see the workmen's wagon pulling away with the men sprawled inside it. Sarah was surveying the finished work done in the study and Millicent halted, struck by the rich beauty of the room, the carved corner posts, and dark wood moldings. Haddington Hall was taking shape more rapidly and more beautifully than she had dared to hope.

"Audrey met Dean Fowler again today," she told Sarah over dinner and quickly repeated the account of this latest episode. "He plainly has something in his craw," she said as she finished. "Perhaps Lady Millicent should give him an audience."

"No, not yet. He might reveal himself yet and save us a lot of unpleasantness," Sarah said. "Meanwhile, I shall continue to inquire about the gentleman, if that is indeed what he is."

"Oh, Sarah, you know he's that, regardless of his high and mighty attitudes," Millicent protested.

"I don't *know* anything yet," Sarah countered. "Besides, Lady Millicent will have enough things to keep her busy. I've planned a visit to the College of Arms tomorrow."

"The College of Arms? What in heavens for?" Millicent asked in surprise, and that was when Sarah brought up the matter of the family coat of arms.

"There has to be one, of course," she said. "I think the Haddington crest would look most elegant on the table linen, the napkins in particular."

Oh, my what a perfectly smashing idea," Millicent agreed, embracing the thought with instant enthusiasm, then at once set upon by a moment of alarm. "But mightn't that be dangerous?" she asked. "Might we not be opening up a proper can of worms?"

"You mean to offer real proof or evidence of your propriety to call yourself Lady Hardesty?" Sarah said. "Yes, I thought about that. They will be asking about and looking into your right to the title of Lady Hardesty, but you are the only family member, however distant."

"Isn't distance quite an important element?" Millicent asked.

"It is, frankly, but they will take so terribly long to investigate that part of it. We shall have succeeded or have failed long before they come to that. If we have succeeded, I daresay they won't press anything at all. So it all still comes down to that," Sarah said. "Meanwhile, the crest will be a very impressive note to add."

"All right, first things first. Mr. Dean Fowler will have to wait," Millicent agreed.

"Remember, Lady Millicent will of course invite him to the grand ball. It would be only courtesy to do so. It might also be the best setting to meet him," Sarah said. "Now get some sleep. We've an early start on hand tomorrow."

Millicent hugged the ample form and hurried up to the large bed. Changed into a lacy nightgown, she lay in the bed to find that thoughts of Dean Fowler persisted in clinging. Her desire to grant him an audience was made of more than propriety and curiosity, she admitted. She wanted a more personal meeting with Dean Fowler, on proper terms. Yet suddenly she found herself wondering how very awkward such a meeting might be now. She had duped him twice and he wasn't the kind of man who would take easily to being played for a fool. The meeting could be more than awkward. It might be disastrous, she realized. Sarah might have been quite right. The best time for him to meet Lady Millicent, and learn the truth, might well be at the formal surroundings of the ball. There were two reasons which dictated that course. She would be at her most lovely that night and public displays of anger would be out of place.

She sighed, and turned on her side. She didn't want to complicate matters before they even got started yet that was precisely what she had done. Not that it took very much to complicate this new world of hers. She closed her eyes finally as sleep, like an insistent suitor, refused to be denied.

The ride to London was pleasant in the morning sun, the great brick building of the College of Arms exuding an air of guarded welcome. Thoroughly appropriate, Millicent thought as she walked through the open doors to be embraced by the austere, somber dignity of the great edifice. Family titles and records dating from 1264 reposed in the vaults of the great building. For centuries, Englishmen had referred to the College of Arms as the Keeper of the Blood, the surpreme arbiter and judge of all matters regarding the rights to heraldic crests and armorial bearings. Their decisions, if need be, were enforced by the Court of Chivalry, Millicent knew, and silently she muttered to herself that she was indeed tilting at some rather formidable windmills.

"Lady Millicent Hardesty and companion," she announced to the gentleman at a desk just to the right of the entranceway. "Here on matters of the family coat of arms," she said loftily. After a short wait on a stone bench, which to her seemed a lot longer than it was, Millicent was ushered into the office of one of the four pursuivants attendant on such matters for the College, the *Rouge Croix* Pursuivant, a very tall, austere-looking gentleman named Ronaldson. Millicent presented her title to Haddington Hall for him to peruse, detailed her relationship to Sir Thomas, and finally signed an oath saying that she was indeed a blood member and direct descendant of the last member of the Haddington family proper. Mr. Ronaldson wrote everything down carefully and slowly in a thick, moroccobound ledger, then disappeared for almost a half-hour to finally return with a parchment of the Haddington family crest.

Sarah whipped out a small notepad and piece of charcoal, and quickly sketched the crest, marking the colors of gules in the first and fourth quarters and argent within. Mr. Ronaldson, speaking with gravity —in fact, Millicent wondered if he ever smiled— addressed her directly. "You realize it will take a considerable time for the College to approve your official use of the crest," he said. "A full and thorough search and documentation of your background must be made and the College will, no doubt, write to you for additional information."

"Yes, of course," Millicent said.

"And you realize, also, that a disapproval will mean you cannot use the coat of arms in any manner whatsoever," he said gravely.

"Naturally, but that is, of course, unthinkable," Millicent said and hoped she sounded a great deal more certain than she felt.

The man nodded and his voice took on a crisper tone for a moment. "Your use of the crest is thereby limited until notice of formal approval is issued," he said. "That is, no public displays, no banners, no emblazonment upon coach doors. Private use only may be made now."

"Of course," Millicent said, rising. "Thank you so much." She swept from the room and out to the waiting carriage, Sarah following on her heels. "Table linen is certainly private use," she commented smugly when they were inside the carriage.

"Indeed," Sarah echoed. "I'll see to the embroi-dery the moment we return." The carriage from the ancient building, threaded its way gate Hill to Fleet Street, down the S Knightsbridge Road, and finally once aga the countryside. The day was nearly gon returned to Haddington Hall and Sarah p ing to the embroidery matter until the follo when she went to Oldham Mews where a Mrs. Appleton did the finest embroidery work in the region. Millicent busied herself with numerous chores in the house and tried not to think about Dean Fowler. It was difficult, indeed impossible, when keeping one eye out the windows in case he should ride up for another try at seeing Lady Millicent. But Sarah's return brought further news of him, information completely without revelation.

"It seems Mr. Fowler and Sir Thomas were often seen together," Sarah announced. "Apparently he was one of the very few people your distant uncle allowed to visit him in his late years."

"Yes, Sir Thomas had become something of a recluse according to Mr. Ackrood's letter, remember," Millicent frowned. "Perhaps that piece of news does explain Mr. Fowler. Perhaps he feels he has the right to ride Haddington Hall land because of the relationship he had with Sir Thomas."

"That doesn't explain all his strange comments, though," Sarah answered and Millicent had to agree. "There's something else in the gentleman's craw," her companion said. "Time will tell, especially if you ____ay from him."

____ent nodded and tried not to look unhappy. ___ Fowler was becoming more and more fas- ___re and a more a figure of mystery. She ___, from the distance of the top dormer ___ a few days later as she was rummaging ___ top floor. She hurriedly fetched her opera glasses and watched him ride the big gray stallion

92

across his land, near the little stream where she'd first met him. He exercised the horse at a fast canter, riding beautifully, one with his mount, and she watched until he rode out of sight. She returned the glasses to her room with a faint sigh. He still seemed everything she had come here to find, right under her nose, as it were, and hoped she wasn't making a mistake by avoiding him.

But the following day brought news of a nature to sweep all thoughts of Dean Fowler away, for the moment, at least. She was talking to Sarah in the newly refurbished grand drawing room, now gleaming and glistening with its burnished gold curtains and pastel blue walls, except for the east wall with its muraled trompe l'oeil scenes, when the sound of a coach drawing up outside made her frown. Howell admitted a coachman in a smart, dark green outfit, who handed Millicent a pink, square envelope, and addressed to her in a flowing, cursive hand. "I am to wait for an answer, m'lady," he said.

Millicent took the envelope into the study and the writing desk, Sarah following, and tore it open at once. She read the bold but lovely handwriting aloud.

Lady Millicent Hardesty
Haddington Hall
Guildford

My Dear Lady Hardesty,

I am taking the liberty of asking you to afternoon tea this Friday the tenth at three. Would you please give my coachman your reply.

Cordially,
The Countess Juillienne de Berrie

Millicent's eyes flew up to Sarah and the older woman motioned with her finger to her lips for silence. She nodded to the writing desk. "Just reply, accepting, of course," she said.

Millicent penned the answer, only a brief two lines:

My Dear Countess,

Thank you so much. I am most honored and shall be there. Lady Millicent Hardesty.

She called Howell in, had him give the envelope to the coachman, and closed the door to the study. In a twinkling, she was dancing in Sarah's arms. "It worked. The cheese worked," she exclaimed.

"Of course. The social scene loves something new and an eligible widow is a wonderful addition," Sarah told her.

"How would the Countess know I am eligible?" Millicent said.

"My dear, I assure you the Countess has been having her people make discreet inquiries, just as I've done regarding Mr. Fowler. By now she knows you are eligible and a widow. But of course, there are eligible chambermaids. It's what she doesn't know that fascinates her," Sarah answered.

Millicent felt her lips tighten for a moment. The first major test was only a few days away. Things had been going so well, but it could all be shattered if she failed in this. Sarah read the thoughts in her suddenly troubled brown eyes.

"I've no fears that you will do anything other than beautifully," Sarah said. "There will be more than the Countess on hand, I should wager."

"Why? How do you know such a thing?" Millicent asked.

Sarah laughed softly. "I know human nature. When you leave, the Countess will want someone there to talk to about the Lady Millicent, good or bad talk. It's no fun unless you can talk to someone afterward."

"Then I shall see that it is good talk," Millicent vowed, lifting her chin.

The next few days were filled with preparations, with reviewing lessons already learned and deciding on attire.

"The maroon dress with the basque bodice," Sarah said. "You want to be very attractive but not stunning. That you'll save for the ball."

Friday came too quickly, almost as though there'd been no days preceding it and at two thirty, Millicent stepped into the clarence, the deep maroon gown softly rich, quietly elegant. Rupert had told her how long the ride to Windsor would take and she timed it to arrive promptly at the appointed hour. When she reached the Countess de Berrie's country residence at Windsor, she found that the house was large, bearing a somewhat ornate and overworked exterior, she thought critically. She felt the smile inside her. Six months ago she wouldn't have had the knowledge to make such an evaluation and now it came almost automatically. Her adventure had already brought unplanned rewards. She alighted from the clarence as the door was opened by a butler.

Her pendant watch read exactly three o'clock when she was ushered into a bright, airy enclosed patio with wrought iron furniture. "Lady Millicent Hardesty," the butler announced in clipped tones Millicent stepped into the room, and swept those there in one quick glance. Sarah had been right again. There were three other women present, but Millicent's glance passed over them to concentrate on the Countess de Berrie, who rose to greet her, lifting a tall frame out of a Queen Anne chair.

Once again, she found how unreliable preconceptions proved to be. She had expected a rather avaricious woman, one who exuded aggressive dominance. She had envisioned a fierce, somewhat beaked face with sharp, darting eyes. The Countess de Berrie's face was not at all sharp or beaked, but quite handsome. Her eyes, blue and very bright, held the hint of a twinkle in them. Her hair, almost blue-white, was carefully styled to add a suggestion of a crown atop her tall frame. She carried a lorgnette in one hand, but didn't use it to survey Millicent with a long, sweeping gaze.

Millicent stepped forward, and extended her hand. "How very nice of you to ask me over," she said.

"I am so glad you could come, Lady Millicent," the Countess de Berrie answered. "Delighted, in fact."

"Oh?" Millicent questioned, tilting her head a fraction to the side.

"Your arrival has set tongues wagging all over," the woman said and her eyes twinkled mischievously. "The social reason has been dismally predictable. We need something new in it. I frankly entertained hopes you might be it."

"I hope I shan't disappoint you, then," Millicent said smoothly, feeling confidence gathering inside her. The Countess de Berrie was not nearly so frightening or imposing as Millicent had imagined she would be, though she was obviously a woman of formidable authority.

"Let me introduce you to my other guests," the Countess smiled, taking Millicent by the arm, a delicate yet thoroughly authoritative touch. "The sisters Upsham," she introduced. "Gloria and Glovina."

Millicent nodded pleasantly to two ladies in their midfifties, both terribly thin, not quite twins but certainly close enough, both with pale, white skins, aquiline noses, and very black hair worn flat against their temples. They even smiled in unison, both somewhat wan smiles, as though it were almost an effort. Their dresses differed only in color, one pale green, the other pale mauve, both of expensive Japanese silk, their skirts gathered around the waistband instead of swept back in the new fashion, with jockey sleeves with their epaulettelike flounces.

"And this is Lady Salisbury," the Countess introduced, turning to the other woman. Lady Salisbury had tightly curled hair of a grayish brown, and a small-featured face that seemed to sniff out for gossip like an inquisitive ferret. She wore a straight-lined merino dress with a close-fitting plush hat which only accentuated the smallness of her features. The woman's eyes darted over her, Millicent noted.

"Well, we have all been wondering just what you'd look like. You're quite a bit younger than we expected," Lady Salisbury remarked.

"And more beautiful," the Countess added. "A young and beautiful widow, now that will certainly enliven the season. You shall have all the eligible bachelors appearing at our every function."

Millicent smiled as she caught the meaning inside the statement, a note that was certainly encouraging, not unlike the happy surprise of finding a center of toffee cream inside an otherwise ordinary bonbon. She sat down at a gesture from the Countess, which just missed being imperious, and the butler appeared with the tea service, all sparkling and gleaming heavy silver and delicate bone china, a pattern of tiny blue buds on an egg white base. A maid followed with a tray of canapes and tea cookies.

"Tell us something about yourself, my dear," Lady Salisbury said, leaning slightly forward in eagerness, her short, small nose all but twitching, Millicent thought. "Your late uncle, Sir Thomas, was hardly part of this social scene, as I presume you know."

Millicent allowed a reluctant smile. "Yes, I'm afraid Uncle Thomas was almost antisocial. It was quite obvious in all his letters." She sat back and took a canape from the maid. *A bit of embroidery wouldn't hurt,* she thought inwardly.

"I am informed you are bringing Haddington Hall back to its former splendor," the Countess said. "You are apparently going at the task in a most thorough manner. I should presume that means you intend staying on at the house."

"Indeed," Millicent said.

One of the Upsham sisters took up the questioning and Millicent wished she could remember which was which. "Your relationship to the Haddingtons is on your mother's side, then," the woman offered.

"Yes, that is correct," Millicent answered and felt a stab of uneasiness. The questions, though cloaked in pleasant conversational good manners, were nonetheless probing. The inquisition was exquisitely disguised. "It is so marvelous to be back in England," Millicent said, seizing the initiative to turn away another probing question. "Unless you have been away for a good while, you just can't appreciate how it feels to return."

"Is is true that you were in Australia?" Lady Salisbury asked, making the name sound faintly odorous.

"Yes, it's true," Millicent answered and managed not to sound defensive.

"Good heavens, my dear," the Countess exploded. "Why would anyone go to that wild place, especially a young woman such as yourself?"

"I went with my husband," Millicent said calmly.

The Countess nodded, put down her lorgnette, and looked slightly less disapproving. "That's different," she said, taking a sip of tea. "Marital obligations can be so burdensome. I had a husband who had an absolute *penchant* for the French provinces. He'd rush me there at every opportunity. I couldn't stand them—so provincial. But at least the food was civilized there," she finished.

One of the Upsham sisters took up the probing, asking her query with a pale smile. "What brought you back here to England, my dear?" The question was couched in a saccharine sweetness. "Not anything so plebeian as simple homesickness, I hope," the woman added.

"That was, plebeian or not, one of the motivating forces," Millicent replied.

"Do I detect something a bit more interesting?" the Countess de Berrie put in, her eyebrows lifting just the right amount for a little more than polite curiosity. "I do know that finding a proper matrimonial prospect is virtually out of the question in a place such as Australia."

Millicent let her smile glow. "That is always a possibility, isn't it?" she parried neatly, letting the Countess make her instant assumptions with smug satisfaction.

"Well, then, we must introduce you to the most eligible and fascinating young bachelors about town. We do have a number of them in London society. It will be fun watching them pursue you and noting which you toss aside out of hand."

"We shall see," Millicent, cryptic, admitting nothing yet implying everything.

"I hoped you might have spent some time on the continent before coming from Australia," the Countess said. "I thirst for some little morsel of gossip from overseas, Spain or France. Even America. There is a line to the colonies that definitely exists. But Australia, that's a wilderness totally out of our London society. By the way, did you know the Aldersons, by any chance? Roger and Clarissa Alderson. He left for Australia some years back."

"Oh, yes," Millicent lied smoothly. Well, it wasn't an absolute lie, she told herself. Sarah had worked for the Aldersons, had come to Australia with them. "I hired my companion, Sarah Elkins, from the Aldersons," she added.

"Ah, yes, Sarah Elkins. She has been employed by some of the best families here. I'm surprised you were able to hire her away from the Aldersons.

Roger always guarded his people so jealously. His sister is still here, you know, married to a bore in Parliament. She keeps telling everyone her brother likes it so in Australia that he's decided to stay there."

Millicent's eyes narrowed a fraction. The Countess so wanted a bit of gossip from afar. She'd give her one and improve her standing at the same instant.

"His sister is not being quite truthful, I'm afraid," Millicent said. The Countess's eyebrows lifted at once and she turned waiting eyes on the younger woman. "Roger Alderson lost everything he had in a gold mine that turned out to have no gold in it," Millicent said. "That's why he's staying on there and that's why I was able to hire Sarah Elkins."

Millicent saw the Countess's eyes light up, her smile becoming one of pure glee. Yet there was no malice in it. The woman simply enjoyed being privy to gossip, to little inside secrets. She reveled in the pleasure of the game. "Now, that alone is worth your visit, my dear," the Countess said. "That is indeed a *bonne bouche*. I always felt Estelle Alderson was, to say the least, careless with the truth. How nice this will be to set in front of her."

Millicent sat back, and sipped her tea as she fended off more questions, turning away those that were difficult, giving out quick sallies of her own. It was a game, all of it, idle pastimes brought to a fine art, and she found herself enjoying the fencing even though she disliked the substance. Lady Salisbury, for all her ferretlike open enthusiasm for gossip, and the Upsham sisters' refined participation, paled beside the Countess de Berrie, who brought an infectious enthusiasm to her role. She didn't try to hide her social power and, despite the veneer of manners, the Countess had a kind of directness that was embracing. Millicent found it impossible not to like the woman despite the shallowness of her pursuits. She glanced at the wall clock with the gilt ornamentation and saw that she should have taken her leave ten minutes ago.

"I fear I've overstayed my welcome," she said, genuine alarm in her voice.

The Countess waved a hand. "Not at all, my dear. I've enjoyed every minute of it," she said.

Millicent decided that a breath of honesty might be refreshing and, she hoped silently, welcome. "I'm glad, then," she admitted. "Frankly, I wanted you to like me."

"Did you, now?" the woman said, fastening a suddenly stern eye on Millicent. Inwardly, Millicent's stomach turned. Had she said the wrong thing? Was honesty simply not part of the game, ever? But she saw the Countess's eyes twinkle, her handsome face break into a smile. "How delightfully frank, my dear," the woman said. "And while we're being so frank, you, of course heard that I rule the social scene with an iron hand."

Millicent allowed a small and rueful smile. "Rather something like that," she said.

The Countess patted her arm in a motherly fashion. "You are a good young woman," she murmured, then swept the other women in the room with a mischievous glance. "They won't say so to you, my dear, but they all know why I rule this little world, if that is indeed true."

"Oh, it's true," Lady Salisbury said with a touch of envy in her voice.

The Countess laughed softly again. "It's no special power, my dear. I'm simply too well entrenched, and too old, to be pulled into all the little cabals and intrigues which are a constant part of the scene. I've no patience with all the *tracasseries* that come along and so my position is one untouched by lesser whirlpools and leaves me to do exactly as I please. They envy that, and naturally pay homage to it."

Once again, Millicent felt the simple, truthful enjoyment in the woman's attitude, an honesty that was at once disarming. She drew her breath in for the question that would tell her exactly how well she had done this afternoon.

"I intend to give a grand ball to celebrate the restoration of Haddington Hall," she said. "I do hope you will come." She half-turned to the others in the room. "All of you, of course," she added.

"I wouldn't miss it for anything," the Countess said. "In fact, my dear, I shall give you the names of some of the most eligible bachelors to invite."

Millicent almost hugged the tall form. She held back at once, but her smile was warm and honest and she didn't hide the gratitude in it. "Thank you, so much, Countess," she said, getting to her feet.

"Nonsense, my dear. I shall enjoy every minute of the season now. But you must promise to keep me informed of your favors and your dislikes, your plans and entanglements. That is my price, to be first with the inside news of the moment."

"I promise," Millicent said. It seemed a harmless enough promise, the tossing out of idle tidbits. Indeed, it was a small price for the Countess de Berrie's approval, she told herself. The butler appeared and, after a round of good-byes to everyone else there, Millicent was shown out. The carriage ride home seemed endless as she felt the excitement whirling inside her. Sarah was waiting when she arrived, drew her into the study, and closed the door.

"It went well," the woman said. "I can see it in your face. Your cheeks are red with excitement."

"It went perfectly," Millicent half-shouted, and hugged Sarah to her. Quickly she told what had happened, recounting every detail that she had engraved onto her mind. When she finished, she sat back, suddenly exhausted.

"You did make an impression, I'd say," Sarah beamed. "We shall prepare for the ball at once. The Countess is obviously on your side, now, which is a great help, but there is still the mainstream of London society. That is where you will find that paragon you want, a man to keep you in riches and in love."

"You make it sound so crass when you put it that way," Millicent said, suddenly feeling annoyed.

Sarah's face bore quiet patience. "Come now, love, isn't that the very way you put it? Isn't that what this is all about?"

Millicent glowered into space, Sarah's words true yet untrue. The question left her lips before she could hold it back. "Anything more from Dean Fowler?" she asked.

"No, though I did see him in the distance. I'd say he was riding Haddington Hall land, though I can't be certain," Sarah answered.

"Let's start readying things for the ball, then. I was looking at the bank balance yesterday. Time is becoming more critical," Millicent said stiffly and knew the state of the exchequer hadn't a thing to do with her remarks. Sarah's quiet smile told her she knew it, also.

"We'd best see to your gowns at once, then," Sarah said.

"Gowns?" Millicent asked at the use of the plural.

"There'll be many invitations for other balls," Sarah said. "You can't be wearing the same gown to them all."

"No, of course not," Millicent agreed. "Shall we go to Edwardson on Bond Street?"

"He'll be too busy to serve you quickly," Sarah replied. "There was a young Frenchman who'd opened a shop just before I left with the Aldersons,

Jacque Donnet, on Regent Street. Let's try him. He was most talented."

Millicent agreed quickly. She had little patience for picking her way through couturiers and tailors and in the morning she set off with Sarah to London. The designer, Donnet, was still there with a greatly expanded shop, according to Sarah. But he was anxious to please, accommodating and, most of all, talented. The day was spent choosing fabrics, styles, initial fittings, and standing very still for long periods while the couturier molded material to her figure. It was enjoyable but tiring and when she returned to Haddington Hall after dark, Millicent went quickly to bed and slept without a thought of Dean Fowler. She woke early, and made a note on her diary pad of the next visit to Jacque Donnet scheduled for a week away.

"You'll have plenty to do meanwhile just preparing the invitations," Sarah told her when she went downstairs. "They must all be personally written, of course."

Sarah handed her a preliminary list of those to be invited and Millicent sat down at the writing desk, beginning the slow task of writing the invitations to be posted together later. She paused as she wrote the one to Dean Fowler and had a moment of apprehension. Perhaps he wouldn't come, she wondered. He did want to see the Lady Millicent but perhaps not in those surroundings. Yet hadn't Sarah been told he was something of a rakehell? Then he'd not turn

107

down an invitation to a ball. She sealed the envelope, having reassured herself that he would attend. She still had to decide how she'd handle the confrontation, but put off thoughts of that for another time.

During the next few days she managed to squeeze in a trip to Windsor and the Countess de Berrie. The woman was delighted to help furnish a list of leading bachelors to be invited. "Sir Craig Emlyn must be at the top of your list," she said. "Family, money, a title, and good looks. What more is there?"

"Not much," Millicent agreed. *Only love,* she added silently, refusing to cast that aside. True, her venture was a calculated move to find material comforts and love, but not the one without the other. Even Sarah failed to grasp that fully. The Countess de Berrie could hardly be able to understand it. Sentimentality was hardly one of the woman's qualities, but Millicent was grateful for the Countess's help and interest and made certain to tell her so.

"Nonsense, my dear. It makes me feel young again and you know how I love being on the inside of anything. Just let me know who you fancy when the time comes," the Countess said.

"You shall be the first to know," Millicent promised. She paused for a second only at the question that flew into her thoughts, then decided to pose it at once. "Do you know anything about a Mr. Dean Fowler?" she asked.

"That handsome Yorkshireman?" the Countess returned.

"Yes, I believe that is he," Millicent said.

"I've seen him at a few events. He cuts quite a figure with the ladies but he's too elusive for any of them to pin down. He's a member of Boodle's and White's, I believe." Millicent recognized the names of two of London's oldest and most prestigious men's clubs. "You've met the gentleman?" the Countess asked.

"He's a neighbor," Millicent said, skirting the question rather deftly, she thought. The Countess walked to the door with her as she prepared to take her leave. "I do hope you will see to your floral arrangements yourself, my dear," the woman said.

"Indeed. I love to arrange flowers. It's one of my talents, if I say so myself," Millicent answered.

"Good. Gardeners arrange well but their bouquets are always entirely too stiff. Servants have a perfect mania for filling every vase too full and eliminating every bit of greenery. I always arrange my own flowers," the Countess said. "I'll see you soon, my dear."

Millicent rode back to Haddington Hall and was quick to tell Sarah that Dean Fowler was a member of both Boodle's and White's. "A sign of breeding and substance, I'd say," she suggested, casting a quick glance at the older woman.

"Possibly," was all Sarah would allow and Millicent gave up trying to shake Sarah's skeptical caution and retired to the study to finish the invitations, adding the new names the Countess had supplied. The days passed with gathering speed. Two more

109

visits to Jacque Donnet brought completion of her wardrobe and the invitations dispatched, some by post and others by messenger. She had Rupert deliver Dean Fowler's and she was waiting when he returned with more anxiety than she wanted to let on.

"Did Mr. Fowler give you an acceptance, Rupert?" she asked.

"Well, yes, he did, after a fashion," the coachman said.

"Meaning exactly what, Rupert?" Millicent pressed.

"He seemed rather irritated, ma'm, when he read the invitation," the man answered. "His jaw tightened and his eyes snapped at me."

"What did he say exactly?"

"He said to tell you he'd certainly be there, ma'm," Rupert told her. "And turned and slammed the door in my face."

"Thank you, Rupert," Millicent said, dismissing the man. She turned away, her brown eyes darkening. *Dean Fowler was irritated, was he,* she thought. Well, she was becoming irritated at his strange remarks and arrogant attitudes. She even felt irritated for Audrey at his high-handed liberties. The Countess de Berrie might yet have some fireworks to talk about when the ball was over, Millicent reflected.

The acceptances began to return in less than a week and by the time Millicent had journeyed to London for a final fitting, all had been received. The final preparations went forward quickly, the extra help for the ball hired and the last-minute touches on the great house finally finished.

"You've done beautifully so far, love," Sarah said to Millicent finally, the night before the night of nights. She and Millicent were alone in the study, the servants all in bed already. "Tomorrow night is the final test."

"Tomorrow night," Millicent breathed in awe. "I can't believe that the moment is really at hand."

"They've all said they were coming, all the cream of London society," Sarah said. "And all eyes will be on you and your grand ball. Even the Countess, much as she seems to have taken a liking to you, will be watching, waiting, listening for a faux pas, a mistake, a blunder. But if the evening is yours, all London will be open for you. All London will be your oyster. You will be able to pick and choose as you wish."

"And find what I want?" Millicent asked quietly.

The older woman's smile held caution. "Ah, my dear, that no one can answer. That will depend on you, on how high you want to reach or on what you're willing to settle for." She rose, yawning, and patted Millicent's arm. "Don't sit here too long. You need your rest. Tomorrow night will be a lengthy one."

Sarah bustled from the room and Millicent sat back in the deep, leather chair. The room grew silent and seemed to encircle her protectively. The lamp cast a small mantle of light around where she sat and

the rest of the room became darkened shapes, clear
yet unclear, as though everything had taken on a
new, unfathomable form. The room and the future
were suddenly alike, clear yet unclear, all taking on
new contours. Only one goal staged sharply etched
in her mind. Millicent's lips tightened for a moment
at the thought. She had come here to win. She had
gambled everything to find what she wanted. She
would settle for nothing less than that. No second
bests, no accommodations, nothing less than love
surrounded by all the other riches she wanted.

She would not let herself fall in love with anyone
but the right person, Millicent told herself sternly,
sitting alone in the silence of the great, darkened
room. She repeated it, an admonition. No one but the
right person, she said, as if love could be willed, as
though the heart ever obeyed anything but itself.

CHAPTER SIX

The time had come. Millicent lay across the bed in only her underskirt and watched the night shadows slip into the room, turning the windows into black squares. She had thought to catnap but everything had passed before her, all that had happened from the first day in Toowoomba to now, pictures of the mind drawn by an unseen hand. So much had come her way because of that decision, a new world, a new life, a grand gamble. She was both frightened and exhilarated.

The time had come.

Millicent rose, and swung her long, lovely legs over the edge of the bed. She sat down before her dressing table and began to prepare for the evening. It did not take long. She needed no elaborate make-up, no heavy powders or wigs, no thickening of the eyebrows or rouge. Her skin glowed of itself, pink-tinted cream, needing only a touch here and there to enhance her natural loveliness. When she finished, she rose, and stepped into her underslip, then the petticoat. The gown was next. Carefully, she took it from the closet and put it on.

Millicent surveyed herself in the mirror and a little smile touched her lips. The gown, a very delicate yellow tulle embroidered with the tiniest of red flowers with a low bodice that pushed her breasts upward —not that she needed any false fullness—and short balloon sleeves, was breathtaking. It combined delicacy and impact, lightness and strength. As she finished adjusting the fit, the sounds of music drifted up from downstairs. A quintet had been engaged to play for the evening, one that was familiar with the newest rigadoons, minuets, waltzes, and tarantellas, and that latest rage from France, the quadrille, introduced to London only a few months before by the Duke of Devonshire. The musicians were preparing, also, she smiled. Sarah would be at her side during the first part of the evening, naming the arrivals for her, staying discreetly in the background for the remainder of the night. Millicent drew in a deep breath, almost came out of the low bodice, pulled herself in, and swept from the room.

Outside, she descended the stairway, looking like a cloud of brilliant yet delicate yellow. Sarah, waiting below, watched with pride, her eyes beaming. "Absolutely magnificent," she breathed when Millicent reached her, and took up her position just inside the doorway to the grand ballroom. The front door of the great house was standing open, Howell and the two extra butlers hired for the evening waiting at the ready to take the guest's capes or coats. Millicent could glimpse outside, and saw the first carriage drive up to a halt, a black, shining coach-and-four. Another carriage, a white phaeton, came up behind it. They were arriving with promptness and eagerness, Millicent saw and, drew a deep breath as a tall, silver-haired man approached in a resplendent evening coat, a much younger woman on his arm. "Sir and Lady Foster," Sarah murmured.

Millicent greeted the pair with a dazzling smile, the words she had memorized and practiced coming easily to her lips. She would say them a hundred or more times during the evening, proper and polite, warm and embracing, her honest smile reaching out to everyone, the young and the old, female and male alike. "Mr. and Mrs. Donald Rumsford," Sarah murmured as a jolly faced man with an equally round wife appeared.

"Welcome to Haddington Hall," Millicent said again. She murmured a few additional words and the couple went on into the ballroom. Others followed quickly, a procession that seemed endless. She'd never remember all the names and faces, Millicent knew, not in one night. The Upsham sisters arrived; Lady Salisbury with her husband, the Earl of Salisbury, a somewhat dour-faced man. A number of young men appeared, most decently handsome, some in the company of aunts, some with obvious lady friends. Each and every one of them devoured the gorgeous Lady Millicent with his or her eyes.

The ball was in full swing and Millicent's presence was demanded on the dance floor and circulating among her guests. "The Countess hasn't arrived," she muttered to Sarah as she prepared to join the guests.

"She's always one of the last to arrive," Sarah said. "She'll be here."

"And there's someone else not here," Millicent said meaningfully.

"I couldn't answer for that one. Go mingle with your guests," Sarah said. "I'll call you when the Countess appears."

"Or anyone else," Millicent said as she moved into the ballroom. A rigadoon was in progress and one of the young bachelors, Robert Asquith, confronted her with a request for the dance. She took his arm and joined the other dancers. He was ecstatically happy, a nice enough young man, good-looking in a somewhat stiff and proper way, his brown hair carefully groomed, his every gesture and remark clothed in propriety. *And dullness,* Millicent sniffed inwardly.

When the dance ended, she was grateful for Lady Salisbury's presence as the woman insisted she talk with other friends of hers. The inquisitive, eager woman kept busy introducing Millicent again to others, and Millicent noted, staying to listen to the questions thrown at her. Lady Salisbury was waiting for a gaffe, Millicent smiled inwardly. She almost had one when a pompous little man named Alexander Carmody threw one of his abrupt questions at her. His speciality was the Bolognese school of painting and the man obviously reveled in entrapping others with his knowledge. But Sarah had prepared her on each of the guests once the acceptances were all in hand.

"The trompe l'oeil is lovely," the man remarked to Millicent. "Reminds me of the Bolognese painters, don't you agree?"

"Yes, in a way," Millicent replied, seeing the Upsham sisters drift over to listen beside Lady Salisbury's inquisitive face.

"You know the Bolognese school?" Carmody said with deceptive casualness.

"Yes," Millicent answered.

The man pounced like a hawk upon a sparrow. It was obvious that he had demolished many a pretender with his little trap. "Which period do you prefer?" he snapped, his eyes glittering.

Millicent paused, almost in hesitation. Two could play at entrapment. "The late one," she replied.

"The late one," he said, his lips drawing back in an avaricious smile. He fairly trembled with glee "Would that be the third or fourth?" he speared.

"The third," Millicent smiled sweetly.

A hint of disappointment crossed his face, but he

117

hadn't finished with his efforts. "That would be the fifteenth century, correct?" he slid out.

"The sixteenth," Millicent said blandly. "When Caracci founded the period. Of course, I feel that Albani, Lenfranco, and Schidone were its best exponents." She flashed a brilliant smile on his shocked countenance and sailed away, a cloud of glorious yellow, shimmering inside as thoroughly as she did outside. She danced a waltz with a young man named Thomas Darby, who was quick to tell her that he was a favorite sales representative for Lloyds of London. She parried his eager suggestion for another meeting, a "picnic" or "afternoon tea." She'd just finished the dance, and was threading her way through admiring glances and compliments when she caught Sarah waving discreetly to her. She reached the doorway of the room just as the Countess arrived, her silver-blue hair set off by a gown of black velvet with the very avant-garde jockey sleeves.

"How very handsome, Countess," Millicent said in honest admiration, seeing the woman's eyes sparkle.

"Almost as handsome as you are beautiful," she returned. A young man waited on her and she turned to him. "Sir Craig Emlyn, my dear," she introduced.

Craig Emlyn was quick to step forward with a half-bow, taking Millicent's hand, and brushing it with his lips. "The Countess did not prepare me for anyone quite so breathtaking," he said.

It was Millicent's turn to nod. He was terribly

good-looking, she saw, devilishly handsome, in fact, but with a smooth-cheeked boyish look, sandy hair, hazel eyes, and even features perfectly balanced in a slightly rounded face. "I shall try to monopolize you all evening," Craig Emlyn smiled.

"And you shall fail," the Countess interrupted. "The other men here will prevent that. So will Carolyn Smythe. She's here, you know."

Craig Emlyn looked rueful but his smile was quick enough to pass over the moment. Millicent recalled Carolyn Smythe, a pretty enough young woman here with her great-aunt, Lady Deborah Smythe. "Come, Craig, dear, your arm," the Countess commanded and Craig Emlyn offered his arm to the older woman.

"Till later," he said to Millicent as he escorted the Countess into the throng of acolytes waiting for her. Millicent stepped into a little anteroom for a moment to adjust the décolletage of her gown, and had started to return to the ball when she saw a figure appear in the doorway, tall with piercing blue eyes that swept over the crowded ballroom. He seemed to fill the doorway as he halted there, his black hair tumbling carelessly over the strong brow. Millicent felt the tug inside her, and saw Sarah standing back, watching. Millicent stepped forward and his glance came to rest on her. She watched his brows come together as he stared at her.

"Mr. Dean Fowler," she smiled. "I'm glad you could come." She saw the uncertainty still in his eyes

119

as he swept her with a glance, his eyes coming to rest again on her face. The frown deepened on his brow and she bestowed a cool smile on him.

"Yes?" she asked with mock innocence.

The piercing blue eyes hardened for a moment, she saw, riveting on her. "Touché," he said quietly, a hint of grimness in his tone. "My compliments, Lady Millicent."

"It wasn't planned," she offered.

He ignored the remark. "Do you often enjoy these little deceits?" he asked, the edged sarcasm unmistakably in his voice. "The bold servant girl," he bit out. "I should have realized," he added.

"Don't disparage yourself, please. I thought I played the role quite convincingly," Millicent sparred.

"My mistake nonetheless," he said wryly. "I should have been more perceptive."

"Oh, but you were quite perceptive," Millicent remarked and saw his eyebrows lift questioningly. "You said, and I believe I recall the exact phrase quite well, that I could be an 'unusually attractive little piece with a bit of work.' You see how right you were?"

Dean Fowler's lips edged a tight little smile and his eyes speared into her. "Touché, again," he murmured. "I was indeed right about that."

"Do I detect a compliment hiding in that sentence, sir?" Millicent asked.

"Perhaps," he returned. "I think I deserve the next dance."

"Deserve?" Millicent questioned.

"You have had your enjoyment. I should be permitted mine," he answered, and she allowed a gracious nod. He could be charming as well as arrogant, but that didn't surprise her. She took his arm as the musicians struck up a waltz and he whirled her into the tempo with masterful ease, making her feel light as a feather gliding in his arms. He made no small talk but his brilliant blue orbs stayed on her, not missing the rise and fall of her breasts as she dipped and turned. It felt good to be in his arms, she admitted readily. The vibrant strength of the man in his very touch sent a quiet excitement through her.

"You have scored a smashing success, it would seem," he said, glancing at the crowd.

"It would seem," Millicent echoed. His lips moved, as though he were about to add something, but then he held back and the waltz came to an end. Millicent saw the two young women approaching with as much haste as the crowded room and propriety would allow. She couldn't recall their names, only that they had come with the elderly banker, Sir Archibald Howser.

"Dean," the one said. "I didn't expect to see you here."

"Nor I," said the other, taller brunette as she rested one hand upon the lapel of his frock coat. "But I'm delighted."

121

Dean turned to Millicent. "You've met Miss Dobson and Miss Wright, I presume," he said.

"Of course." Millicent smiled, names springing back to her. "Ann Dobson and Miss Cynthia Wright, I believe."

Both young women gave her perfunctory smiles and Millicent heard someone calling, and turned to see the Countess nearby. "Lady Millicent, my dear," the Countess called again.

"Excuse me for a moment," Millicent said to Dean and the two young women. As she turned away she heard Cynthia Wright's voice, a slight petulant edge to it.

"The next dance is mine, Dean," the young woman said. Millicent forced herself not to glance back and hurried to where the Countess waited, Craig Emlyn beside her.

"Dance with the boy, my dear, before he drives me insane," the Countess ordered.

"My pleasure," Millicent replied as the music began again. Craig Emlyn guided her onto the dance area and she found he was a most skillful dancer. His boyish handsomeness made him look younger than he actually was, she decided.

"You had best keep every evening free from now on," he told her. "I shall be at your door constantly."

"My, how impetuous," Millicent laughed, though it was not a quality she would have ascribed to Craig Emlyn.

122

"Not at all, simply captivation," he answered. "Besides, you'll need someone to squire you about."

"Perhaps," she conceded.

"We can do all London town," he said. "We can do whatever you wish." He dropped his voice a tone. "I even know some jolly good bawdy places if you've a mind."

"And what makes you think I've a mind for that sort of thing?" Millicent asked in mock sternness. "Or do you fancy all widows have a mind for that?"

"No, no," he said quickly. "I've just discovered that many young ladies have more of a taste for it than one would suspect."

"Well, we shall see, Sir Craig," Millicent answered.

"Craig. Please call me Craig," he said.

"All right, *Craig,*" she agreed. "But I fear I've so much to do that I'll have few evenings free."

"Nonsense. We shall do each and every one of your errands together," he said and Millicent had to laugh with him. Craig Emlyn combined a sophistication with an eager-puppy enthusiasm that was quite beguiling. He also was quite able to carry on a conversation by himself with only a nod needed from her and she had the moment to find Dean Fowler with her eyes. He danced with Cynthia Wright with what seemed a distant politeness. Or was she only hoping that, she muttered silently, returning her attention to Craig.

When the dance ended, Thomas Darby was there

to claim the next one, Herbert Featherstone waiting to mark the following one for himself, and so it went during the entire evening. Craig Emlyn somehow managed to corner the lion's share of her time, she noted, and he was a most companionable fellow, she decided. She found not a moment free of someone wanting to talk with her or dance or simply enjoy her company. But in between those who vied for her attention she continued to catch sight of Dean Fowler, dancing with various young women at the affair. She had found a moment to sip a glass of punch and catch her breath when the deep, mellifluous voice sounded at her elbow and she turned at once to meet the bright blue eyes.

"I must take my leave, now," Dean Fowler said. "Thank you for having me."

"I'm sorry we could not talk more," Millicent answered. "The circumstances were not propitious."

"Naturally not," he agreed.

"You obviously have wanted to talk to me of something," Millicent said.

"Yes," Dean Fowler said and she saw the piercing blue eyes harden for an instant. "May I come by tomorrow?" he asked.

"I fear tomorrow will not be appropriate," Millicent objected quickly. "I'm sorry, but I shall be exhausted." It was not an excuse. She wanted to be at her very best for this first personal visit from him. "The day after, please," she asked.

"As you wish," he nodded and his lips were

touched by a sudden smile. "I trust Lady Millicent will see me this time," he said.

"She promises," Millicent said.

"Good. I look forward very much to our meeting," Dean Fowler told her.

"I, too," Millicent said, casting aside polite pretenses and matching his honesty. He bowed, brushed her hand with his lips, and turned on his heel to stride away at once. She watched him make his way through the crowd, tall and ramrod straight, somehow detached from everything around him. She half-wished she were going with him. He disappeared through the door and she returned her attention to the ball and Craig Emlyn hovering nearby.

The night moved swiftly and as the hour grew late, the revelers began to drift away. The Countess de Berrie took Millicent aside at one point. "Craig is getting my cape and he will escort me home, of course," the woman said. "It was a perfectly lovely ball. Just remember, you'll keep me informed of any romantic developments. Or any other intriguing ones."

"You have my word," Millicent said. "Thank you for helping to make it a success."

"Not at all. I like successful affairs," the Countess said. "Of any kind," she added with a twinkle. Millicent bid Craig Emlyn good night and received a vow to pursue her with enthusiasm. Finally, in the small morning hours, the last guest had gone home, and the extra help had been paid and sent on their way.

The magnificent front door closed for the last time and the great house fell silent. Millicent went upstairs to her bedroom, stripped down to an underslip, and doused her face with cold water. She'd just finished drying herself when Sarah stopped in and Millicent clasped her arms around the ample form in happy exhaustion.

"You did it, my dear," the older woman said. "It was a grand success. Not a *coup manqué* the entire evening."

"It went more beautifully than I'd dared to hope," Millicent agreed. "Thanks to all your work."

"But it was you who had to carry it off. They came, they saw, and you conquered," Sarah beamed as Millicent allowed herself the warm glow of satisfaction. "What did you think of Sir Craig Emlyn?" Sarah asked. "He's certainly a charming, witty companion. Terribly attractive, too."

"Yes, he's all that," Millicent thought aloud. "But I wonder if it's all surface."

"There is a bit of the carpet knight about him," Sarah agreed. "But with his money, it's unimportant. Did your Dean Fowler have anything to say about his strange behavior and odd remarks?"

"Not a word," Millicent replied. "But he's coming to visit. I had the feeling he was quite taken with Lady Millicent. I'm sure he'll reveal more about himself when he visits next."

"Let's hope he's less abrupt than usual," Sarah said. "Now get to sleep. You should have no trouble

126

doing that tonight. Sleep late. There's no reason to wake early."

Sarah bustled off, closing the door behind her and Millicent finished undressing, slipped into a soft nightgown, and stretched out between the silk sheets. The first great step was done with, passed with flying colors. She was too exhausted to think about anything more. Tomorrow would wait with all its promises.

CHAPTER SEVEN

Millicent slept late the next day and woke still feeling exhausted. She did little more than rest the remainder of the day. "This being the grand hostess is quite enervating," she grumbled to Sarah.

"True enough. Get to bed early tonight. I daresay you'll be receiving numerous invitations and callers the rest of the week. Craig Emlyn will no doubt head the list," Sarah opinioned.

"No doubt," Millicent agreed as thoughts of only one caller stayed in her head as she went up to her room to sleep. In the morning, she woke feeling herself, and had just dressed and breakfasted when Dean Fowler arrived. He was clothed in a gray morning jacket with a white scarf curled around his neck and he looked terribly dashing. Millicent was glad she hadn't put on an ordinary housedress, but chosen the deep-blue gown with the flat-pleated sleeves and loose bodice.

"I'm too early," Dean Fowler said, catching the moment of surprise in her face as Howell showed him into the house.

"Not too early, just early," Millicent replied, recovering from her surprise. He did not smile but the strong intenseness of his face held her eyes. "Let us go into the study," she said. "It's always quiet and comfortable there."

He followed her into the warm, wood-paneled room and she saw his glance sweep her gown in one quick motion, pausing a moment appreciatively on the full rise of her breasts, and moving to the auburn tints of her hair set aglow by the sun through the tall window. "Do you always look so ravishing in the morning?" he asked, still unsmiling.

"That's for others to decide," she answered. His eyes stayed on her, piercing, evaluating. The imperiousness was in his face again, though without the condescension there had been with Audrey. "Your beauty makes it difficult to concentrate on the business that has brought me here," he commented.

She felt her frown dig into her brow. "You sir, have the somewhat dubious talent of making a compliment sound uncomplimentary," Millicent remarked. He said nothing but she saw the brilliant blue eyes narrow a fraction. "You say business brought you here?" Millicent went on. "I had thought this a visit of a more personal nature."

She watched as his lips pursed before he answered. "My apologies, then," he said. "I should very much like to pay such a visit to you. I had hoped to perhaps combine the two."

"Well, that's a bit better," Millicent said and surprised herself at how coolly regal she sounded. His presence was making her feel anything but cool. "What business could you possibly have to discuss with me?" she asked.

"The purchase of Haddington Hall," he answered brusquely.

"The what?" Millicent blurted.

"The purchase of Haddington Hall," he repeated. "I wish to purchase the house and the lands."

Millicent knew she was staring at him. "Purchase Haddington Hall? You can't be serious," she said. Then, peering at the intensity of his handsome face, she added, "You are serious, aren't you?"

"Completely," he said.

Millicent continued to stare at him as she tried to gather in her whirling thoughts. Haddington Hall was not only integral to her plans but she had developed a terrible affection for the great house. Bringing it back to its glory had made her feel a part of its heritage, as though she had always belonged here.

"Absolutely unthinkable," she snapped out.

Dean Fowler's eyes hardened. "Do hasty, ill-con-

131

sidered answers come naturally to you?" he returned.

"Not as easily as arrogance comes to some people," she shot back.

The burning blue eyes stayed on her and then suddenly softened, growing light with wry amusement. "The thrust and parry of a master swordsman and beauty, besides. You have too much of an advantage, my dear Lady Millicent," he said. She let her glare fade away. "I shall rephrase my request. I ask you to entertain my offer to purchase Haddington Hall and to bear in mind the material benefits from such a sale. Is that better?" he said.

Millicent smiled inwardly at her small victory. He wasn't so intimidating at all when one faced up to him. But he was still sweepingly attractive. "I shall think on it," she said loftily. "That is all I'll say on the matter for now."

He nodded. "Then we shall begin our meeting again on that more personal level," Dean Fowler said. "I must be in London this afternoon. Following a business meeting, I shall attend a small dinner at an aunt's town house. I should be honored if you'd be my guest for dinner. There won't be more than four or five people. I shall send my carriage for you."

Millicent's mind clicked off thoughts. Dean Fowler was taken with her. The heart has its own wisdoms. Such things can be read in a glance, in a moment, the unstated chemistry that passes between a man and a woman. Yet he wouldn't be above

132

tempting to charm her into agreeing to his objectives, she was aware and she smiled inwardly. Two could play at the game of charm. She had her own weapons, perhaps far better ones than his. Besides, she did want to know more about this fascinating man. What better way to begin to find out than at a small dinner party? she asked herself.

"Thank you, I think that might be most pleasurable," she answered.

"I'll have the carriage pick you up at seven o'clock, then," he said, getting to his feet. He seemed genuinely pleased. "Till tonight." He half-bowed and left at once. Millicent stayed for another moment alone in the study, still feeling the electricity of his presence and turning the strange twists of the morning's events over in her mind. When she finally rose and went into the hallway, Sarah was waiting. Millicent quickly told her what had transpired and of the evening's impending dinner engagement. "You're not excited at all," Millicent complained as she saw Sarah's slightly jaundiced glance.

"Be careful, my dear. You could be playing a dangerous game," the older woman said. "You're quite taken with him."

"Dangerous?" Millicent bristled, dismissing the word instantly. "Nonsense. I shall enjoy winding Mr. Dean Fowler around my finger."

"One can be trapped in one's own web," Sarah insisted.

Millicent thought for a moment. "Perhaps it

133

would be worth it," she returned. "Perhaps I've found what I came to find right under my very nose, Sarah."

"We shall see," Sarah said, letting the weight of years and experience hang on her words.

But Millicent was not to be taken down at all, her mood too full of excitement. "Everything is going beautifully, Sarah," she said. "It will continue to do so. I shall see to that."

She went upstairs, removed the gown, donned a work smock, and spent the rest of the morning in the garden. During the midafternoon, she rested and let the remainder of the day pass on wings. The carriage arrived promptly at seven, a royal blue barouche with an enclosed cab, and she folded herself into its dark privacy, sitting back as it rolled away. She would view Dean Fowler's intense attractiveness from a distance, keeping complete charge of the evening and, in particular, her own emotions. Cool and calm, she repeated again. It was merely a matter of self-discipline.

At precisely eight o'clock, the carriage rolled to a halt in front of a lovely town house in the heart of London, a white-painted door with a gaslight lamp over the center, a black cast iron knocker contrasting effectively with the simplicity of the door. Millicent alighted from the carriage with the help of the driver, mounted the steps, and had not yet lifted the iron knocker when the door opened and a butler showed her into a wood-paneled foyer. She saw Dean coming out to meet her, clothed in an elegant evening coat of royal blue with a high white collar and white ruffled shirt. His eyes took in the soft line of her rounded décolletage as she gave the butler her cape, her dress a soft velvet maroon, full-length with no sleeves.

"How beautiful you look," he said with more than passing gallantry. He offered his arm and led her into a brightly lighted dining salon where two gentlemen and a graciously smiling woman were standing at a beautifully set table. "My aunt, Madam Cornelia Fowler," Dean introduced.

The woman, tall and handsome without being imposing, gestured to a chair. "Dean said he was having a most lovely guest and he was more correct than ever," she said. Millicent smiled in reply, and sat down as Dean held the chair for her. He introduced the two gentlemen, both in their fifties, a Mr. Hannover and a Mr. Treadwell.

"Both gentlemen of commerce," Dean said as he made the introductions. "A polite nod occasionally will be enough attention for them."

"Hardly, you young rake," Mr. Hannover said. "You'll not keep such charming company all to yourself for the entire evening."

Good-natured and friendly banter was obviously part of the relationship and Millicent felt herself relaxing in the warm atmosphere. Dean looked resplendently handsome and she felt her skin tingling, her heart developing a sudden thump. So much for

135

maintaining a cool and calm demeanor, she told herself. She had only meant outwardly, she added, excusing her rush of feelings. She let her eyes enjoy the beauty of the tall-ceilinged room, the table of highly polished satinwood veneer. Red roses in a large cut glass vase added an explosion of color to the quiet elegance of the crystal and white linen place mats.

But most of all, Millicent felt herself enveloped by the magnetic, intense personality of the man beside her. "I'm glad you could come this evening," he said simply.

"Thank you," Millicent returned. "I looked forward to coming." Honesty seemed a proper note for the evening instead of the fencing of the morning meeting, and it effected a change of atmosphere that was rewarding. Her direct questions soon had Dean Fowler talking about himself and the things he held important.

"I hear you've ambitious breeding plans for our English horses," Millicent remarked.

"Ambitious? Perhaps. I suppose that is a good word for it. I'm trying to develop a horse that will be fit for both farm work and comfortable riding. No jumper, mind you, but a good, steady seat for the average rider yet sturdy enough to do a farm horse's ordinary work," he told her.

"A tall order, I should say," Millicent answered.

"Perhaps. It will take good breeding and proper raising of my stock. You do ride, I presume, Lady Millicent," Dean Fowler said.

"I think, 'Millicent' would be in order," she replied. "And yes, I do ride."

"Millicent," he said slowly, savoring the name. "It has a nice sound to it, feminine yet not frothy. Rather like its owner," he said. "You will no doubt be the hit of this social season. How many invitations have you gathered already?"

"A few."

"There'll be many more," he said.

"You sound almost rueful, Dean," Millicent slid out.

His laugh was quick. "Perhaps I am," he said.

"You're welcome to join," she remarked.

"I've never been one for standing in line," he answered.

Her eyes tantalized him, little lights of laughter dancing inside them. "Shy reticence? I hadn't thought that to be one of your traits," she said.

"It isn't," Mr. Hannover cut in. "Dean has never been the fainthearted type. I don't know what's prompted this caution." The man laughed and she saw Dean cast a quick glance at him, a smile edging his lips.

"A slight case of awe, perhaps," he said. He raised his wine glass to Millicent. "To an object quite worthy of awe, a toast," he said.

Millicent lifted her own glass, sipped the wine, and felt the smooth warmth of it slide down her throat. "I once heard that the toast takes its name from the old custom of actually placing a piece of toast in a tankard of ale," she said.

"So it does," Dean replied. "The custom still prevails at Oxford and the other universities. It's said that a gentleman once pledged his honor with a glass of water taken from the bath of a beautiful woman when someone else cried out that he'd have none of the liquid but he'd have the toast that had been in the liquid."

"Which would you have had?" Millicent prodded mischievously.

"Both," he said deftly and she laughed with him as the dessert plates were brought in. The great French chef, Carême, was still creating sixty-course dinners for the Prince Regent at Brighton and chefs everywhere were imitating some of his innovations; *pieces montees,* table decorations that were edible; *poulet* larded with truffles; and aspic molds of tremendous proportions. Madam Fowler's chef had succumbed to the Carême influence in his *entremets,* spun sugar desserts fashioned in the shape of arches and arabesques and as delicious to the tongue as to the eye. Millicent was never so sorry to see an evening end, but not merely for its warmth and elegance. Dean Fowler had proved to be a man of intellect as well as charm and she had begun to wonder if perhaps his imperious air was not without justification.

"Do you care for the arts?" he asked her as the carriage finally took them back to Haddington Hall.

"I spend a good part of my free time at Covent Garden. I especially love the opera. I'm going next week to hear the new work by the Italian, Rossini. It's called *Tancredi*. It was first performed only a few months ago in Venice."

"I'm sure you'll enjoy it," Millicent said.

"There's not another ticket to be had or I'd ask you to accompany me," he explained. Millicent let her hand rest on his arm for a moment.

"Some other time, perhaps," she said.

His hand came with an answering touch upon hers. "Most definitely," he said. He didn't draw his hand back and she made no move to withdraw hers. Only when the carriage halted before Haddington Hall did he remove his hand and the warmth of it stayed with her. His lips brushed her hand as she left the coach, then lingered, the subtlest of messages, yet unmistakable. She went into the house feeling warm, filled with an inner glow. She saw Sarah and the huge bouquet of flowers at the same instant.

"They're gorgeous," Millicent gasped. Sarah handed her the card. Millicent opened it, and read aloud: "To the most beautiful hostess ever . . . Craig Emlyn."

"They came soon after you left," Sarah told her. The flowers were indeed beautiful and Millicent felt a rush of warmth for Craig Emlyn's gracious gesture. He had his own ways of endearing himself. She turned, catching Sarah studying her face.

"The evening went well, obviously," the older

woman said. "You're pleased and smug as a Cheshire cat."

"Oh, indeed. It went smashingly," Millicent replied, hugging Sarah impetuously. "He's really quite wonderful, everything I want, everything any woman could want."

"No arrogance?" Sarah questioned.

"Just a touch. I wonder if it's a defense. For all his reputation as a rake, he was quite proper and I remember when he danced with Cynthia Wright at the ball he seemed actually distant," Millicent thought aloud.

"That often merely means a man has had his fill of a young lady," Sarah said.

"What a crass thing to say!" Millicent protested.

"Crass but often all too true," Sarah rejoined.

"Well, he shan't feel that way about me," Millicent flounced.

"Just don't be too willing. Haste is unseemly but, more importantly, it robs men of their enjoyment. If they win too easily, it robs their prize of value. They need to feel they've conquered."

"All the while it is exactly the opposite," Millicent added.

"Precisely," Sarah said.

"I know he's attracted to me," Millicent said. "Perhaps I've no need to look further."

"Aren't you running off a bit so soon, my dear?" Sarah asked and Millicent made a face and knew her companion was right. "Don't commit yourself. Wind them all around your finger, first," Sarah advised.

"Yes," Millicent agreed, kissed Sarah's cheek, and hurried upstairs. She undressed quickly in the dark and slipped between the sheets. She went to sleep wondering why she didn't really want to heed Sarah's advice though it was the very core of her plan. She refused to consider the answer and embraced the refuge of slumber.

The morning brought a warm sun and another beautiful bouquet of flowers. This time the accompanying note was a request. "Choose any evening, the sooner the better. I grow despondent waiting," she read to Sarah.

"He should have his evening," Sarah said. "All of them deserve at least one until you narrow down the field. You must give them all a fair chance. Most of all yourself."

Millicent smiled at the last sentence. Sarah paused at the door. "I was looking at the account book this morning. You've no need to feel pressed yet, but it is important that you do not limit your sights to one prize," she said.

"I shall follow your advice," Millicent said.

"Good," Sarah said happily.

"But one a little tighter than the others," Millicent finished with a quick laugh as Sarah went off, shaking her head in mock exasperation. The day passed uneventfully and Millicent welcomed the quiet, though she had half-expected Dean to visit. The hope was answered the following morning, though hardly in the way she anticipated. She was in the drawing room, the double doors open, when Howell entered.

"Mr. Dean Fowler to see you, m'lady," the butler said.

"Please show him in," Millicent said, rising and glimpsing Sarah passing in the hallway. Dean appeared a half-moment later, his glance taking in the pale-peach muslin gown that set off her auburn-tinted hair and lay lightly on the swell of her breasts. "Good morning, Dean," Millicent said brightly.

Dean Fowler's eyes studied her with detached interest. "Is there no time when you're not lovely?" he remarked without a smile, only wry admiration in his face.

"Compliments. A perfect way to begin a visit, especially an unexpected one," Millicent said.

"Good, because I've come on something more than a social call. I've come to see you about my offer for Haddington Hall," he said. "You've thought further on it, I presume," he said.

"Yes," Millicent lied for she really hadn't given it any thought at all. The matter had been pushed completely out of her mind and that was a kind of answer in itself, she reflected. "But I see we have returned to paying business calls," she remarked tartly.

"For the moment," he answered. She ignored the unsaid promise in his reply and felt irritation gathering inside her at the imperiousness of his waiting eyes.

"I'm afraid I do not intend selling Haddington Hall in the foreseeable future," she said coldly, then softening her tone. "I'm sorry," she added.

She saw Dean Fowler's strikingly handsome face darken. "And I'm afraid you've no choice," he said.

"No choice?" Millicent frowned, trying not to show the fear that suddenly rushed through her. She groped for words, wanting to demand an explanation yet suddenly afraid to ask. She had visions of everything she'd planned suddenly collapsing around her, her house made of cards that topple over. He saved her the problem of finding words as he reached into his jacket, pulled out a letter, and handed it to her.

"Please read this," he said stiffly. She took the letter, unfolded it, and let her eyes move across the precise penmanship, every letter neatly formed, an old-style script full of curlicues and flourishes.

My Dear Dean,

Your visit the other evening was most stimulating and I am very interested in your work and breeding program. Regarding the things we discussed, this letter will serve to clarify the conversations.

Of course, my will stipulates that Haddington Hall should remain in the family. However, as there is no family in actuality, save for some distant relative scattered someplace, the clause

143

is hardly more than a gesture there only out of a sense of propriety to family heritage.

I am in accord with selling Haddington Hall you which would of course remove the house as part of my estate and render that clause in the will null and void.

This letter will serve as a memorandum of our conversation and my intent.

Respectfully,
Sir Thomas Haddington

Millicent read the key phrases again, then finally looked up, and handed the letter back to Dean Fowler. He clipped out his words: "Unfortunately, Sir Thomas died before he had time to complete the sale of Haddington Hall to me. However, his intent and our agreement is absolutely clear in this letter. Your solicitor's notification to you was a legal formality. I believe he was as shocked as I when you wrote back your intention to retain Haddington Hall."

"I didn't receive that impression from Mr. Ackrood," Millicent answered, not really certain just what impression she had about the solicitor. "I'm sorry, Dean, but I don't see how Sir Thomas's letter affects my ownership of Haddington Hall."

"That letter is a promise, Millicent," he shot out angrily."

"But Sir Thomas is gone. Whatever his intentions

might have been, they are not mine," Millicent returned.

"By God, I expect you to honor the promise in this letter!" Dean said, waving the piece of paper in the air.

Millicent felt her irritation turning to resentment, the feeling pushing aside relief that all Dean Fowler had was the letter. "I don't feel at all obligated to honor that letter," she said crisply. "I see no reason why I must, or even should, be bound by a promise made by a man in his near dotage, perhaps made while he was in his cups."

"The letter is perfectly clear and responsible," Dean insisted angrily. "His intent is absolutely clear —to let me purchase Haddington Hall."

"I see now why you rode Haddington Hall land as though you already owned it, surveying and measuring as if it were actually yours," Millicent said. The piercing blue eyes burned into her without comment, an answer of itself. "Was all this the reason for the other evening, Dean? Was it all just an attempt to charm me into doing what you want?"

"No, it wasn't," he snapped.

"I'm not disposed to believe that, now," Millicent said.

"Believe what you will," he flung back. "The fact is that I need Haddington Hall and its lands for my work and Sir Thomas agreed to let me have it. I expect that promise to be honored."

"Then your expectations are to be dashed, I'm afraid," Millicent returned.

Dean Fowler exploded in fury. "Dammit, you inherited that commitment when you inherited Haddington Hall," he almost shouted.

"Nonsense. I inherited nothing of the sort. You are simply trying to surround a vague intention with all sorts of high-flown words," Millicent returned.

"Words such as honor, integrity, moral responsibility, all things the Lady Millicent seems to have no regard for at all," he countered.

"I think you may leave, now," Millicent said, moving to the doorway. Dean stuffed the letter into his pocket, his eyes blazing, and brushed past her as he strode away, his handsomeness enhanced by his fury. He paused at the front door to glare back.

"I have a promise and I shall insist you honor it," he said.

"Insist? An arrogant word for an arrogant man," Millicent snapped. Dean's jaw twitched as he spun on his heel and strode from the house. Millicent turned to see Sarah there.

"I'd not say you've wound him terribly well around your finger," the older woman commented blandly.

"Did you hear all of it?" Millicent said, her cool discipline dissolving into dismay. "It was perfectly awful."

"I couldn't help hear it," Sarah said.

"It's torn apart everything," Millicent cried. "Was I wrong?"

"Of course not. Your interests are paramount, now, not Sir Thomas's. Mr. Dean Fowler is attempting to make you feel guilty, that's all. Don't let him," Sarah said.

"I certainly won't," Millicent said.

"Forget about him. There are plenty of others for you," Sarah said.

"There certainly are," Millicent agreed. Her brown eyes dark with anger, she strode to the writing desk, sat down, and placed a sheet of stationery in front of her. She needed but a moment to compose the note.

My dear Craig,

Any evening next week would be fine. I'd enjoy going to hear the new Rossini opera. In any case, please inform me as to time, place, and your arrangements.

She paused for a moment before signing, started to put down *Lady Millicent,* and decided to sign *Millicent.* Propriety could take a back seat to encouragement. She showed the note to Sarah and put it into an envelope, sealing the flap with her tongue. "That's putting an end to thoughts about Mr. Dean Fowler," Millicent sniffed.

"Is it, now?" Sarah commented. Millicent ignored

her tone and gave the note to Rupert to post at once. She busied herself during the next few days preparing a plan for a new garden along the west wing of the house and deciding on the parade of invitations that began to arrive each day. After conferring with Sarah, she chose a salon musical at Lord and Lady Dunwood's, a dinner party at the Kerrigans, and a ball at the Upsham sisters. The others she turned down with proper reasons and carefully worded regrets. To accept too many would be unwise and unseemly, Sarah reminded her. But when the invitation from the Countess de Berrie arrived by personal messenger, she quickly accepted. The Countess was sponsoring an art exhibit featuring the latest works of John Constable. She wouldn't have any time at all to think about Dean Fowler, Millicent told herself as she kept thinking about him.

The note from Craig Emlyn finally arrived and she tore it open at once. "He has them," she called delightedly to Sarah, "The tickets for the new Rossini opera."

"I didn't know you were such a devotee of the opera," Sarah remarked. "In fact, I don't remember your ever having mentioned opera to me."

"You don't know *everything* about me," Millicent returned and quickly strode away. It was the next day when, having taken the carriage to Roxbury, she saw Dean on his gray stallion leading a string of six horses. In the bright afternoon sun she saw his eyes, a flash of blue, peer across the field at the carriage.

148

She couldn't be certain whether he saw her or not, but he had to have recognized the clarence and she sat very straight, turning to look back only when he rode on his way. She didn't see him again until a few evenings later when she found herself at Covent Garden on Craig Emlyn's arm.

The opera was as much a social event as it was a musical one. Almost everyone who'd been at her own ball was there, including the Countess de Berrie, who winked at her as she saw Craig. Millicent tried not to spend too much time trying to pick out Dean and succeeded only in not being obvious about it. She grew annoyed as she failed to find him in the huge throng and wondered if perhaps he hadn't come at all. Craig proved to be a witty and delightful conversationalist, perhaps a bit superficial yet always entertaining. He scattered compliments about as though they were confetti and yet managed to make each one sound spontaneous and sincere.

"You are a most wonderful end to a day in Throgmorton Street, Millicent," he told her.

"Do you spend a lot of time in the financial world?" she asked.

"Only when I must see to family business. Father does most of it, thank heaven. When are you going to come meet the family?" he asked. Her quick flash of surprise came before she could hide it. "Think I'm rushing it a bit, do you?" he laughed and looked terribly young. "Perhaps I am but I don't believe in

149

being late for sailing, dinners, or beautiful women," he said.

"Thank you," she smiled, "though I'm not certain I like being put in with sailings and dinners."

"I can't imagine why not," he said with mock dismay. "You transport people and you look positively edible."

She had to join his infectious laughter as the music began again to cut off further conversation. At the close of the second intermission she spied Dean in the front row of a box, looking terribly handsome and tall in his black evening jacket. She felt genuine surprise stab at her as she saw that he was alone. She was still frowning at that unexpected note as the curtain rose for the final act.

When the opera ended, there was a crush of people in the grand lobby. An impromptu party formed as everyone exchanged opinions on the opera and prattled about all manner of things. Suddenly, as Craig was engaged in conversation with the Countess for a few moments, Millicent found herself face-to-face with Dean. His eyes looked down at her with a trace of amusement and she felt her irritation spiral at once.

"I hope you enjoyed the opera," he remarked.

"I did," she snapped. "It seems there were tickets to be had," she added tartly.

"Some people have better connections than others," he answered mildly. His eyes drifted down to the dark-blue gown with the square neck, and the rise of her breasts over the lace at the collar line. The quiet amusement stayed in his eyes, which returned to her face. "You look most lovely," he remarked almost brusquely.

"You're doing it again," Millicent said and his eyes widened in question. "Giving compliments and making them sound as coldly detached as an agricultural report."

"My idiosyncrasy, I expect," he said. "Good night, Millicent," he added curtly, turning on his heel and making his way through the crowd. She was still staring after him when she felt Craig's hand at her elbow.

"Let's have a brandy before the drive back."

She went with him quietly, letting him hold her hand as he led the way out of the theater. During the carriage trip back to Haddington Hall Craig took her hand in his. "It's been more than simply a lovely evening," he told her. "I should like to do it again tomorrow night but I don't suppose that's in the cards, is it?"

"No, it isn't. I need time in between all your attentions," Millicent protested lightly. "You could turn a girl's head."

"I hope so," he answered. "Dare I ask for the following evening?"

"Sorry, I'm attending a dinner party at the Kerrigans," Millicent told him.

"Hang it. I won't be there," Craig snapped. "Can't stand the people. I turned down so many invitations they stopped sending them to me and this is the first time I've wanted one."

"Life is full of small ironies," Millicent remarked. "I'll just have to make the best of the evening on my own."

"Hah!" Craig burst out. "Not hardly likely. Reggie Van Alstine always attends the Kerrigan's affairs. He'll be clinging to you like a wet leaf."

Millicent glanced at the terrible dismay on Craig's face as the carriage halted before the manor house. He was really quite appealing. Impulsively, she leaned forward, and brushed his cheek with her lips as she quickly left the carriage. She turned to see his eyes alight with happiness. "Next Monday?" he asked.

She nodded. "Next Monday," she agreed, and hurried into the house with Craig's shout of exuberant joy following after her. It had been a splendid evening and she went to bed tired but pleased. Relaxing under the smooth, silky sheets, letting her body breathe without even a peignoir over it, she found Dean Fowler suddenly in her thoughts again. He had shown that he was not the least bit upset over their last meeting. She had expected some sort of apology from him for his rude display of anger. Expected? The word caught at her. She'd *wanted* more than *expected* an apology, she admitted. She closed her eyes and went to sleep, refusing to wonder why that brief meeting with Dean stayed in her thoughts more than the rest of the entire evening.

In the morning, Sarah was waiting breakfast for her, full of eager questions about the evening. "Craig is much more aggressive than I'd expected," Millicent told her. "And much more appealing," she added honestly.

"But?" Sarah asked, picking up the unsaid.

"Why do you ask that?" Millicent returned.

"It's in your voice, something unfinished," Sarah said.

Millicent let her face wrinkle. "I suppose I simply must grow accustomed to everything being so glibly on the surface in this social strata," she answered. "Even sincere comments take on an air of superficiality."

"There's nothing superficial about Craig Emlyn's family fortune," Sarah said.

"No, I suppose there's not anything of the kind about Craig, either. It just appears that way," Millicent thought aloud.

"Give him time, that's all," Sarah advised and Millicent nodded in agreement, turning her thoughts to her breakfast. After all, she had come here, created this tremendous gamble on the certainty that she could find someone she could love in this world of high society. It actually seemed far easier than she had expected, the number of attractive young men in greater supply than she'd imagined.

"It's all gone terribly well, hasn't it?" she asked of Sarah.

"Absolutely," Sarah agreed. Millicent nodded and

was quietly annoyed at herself for suddenly needing reassurance.

The days that followed were full and long. The Kerrigan's dinner party was boringly pleasant and Reggie Van Alstine did cling like wet leaf, but Millicent was glad for his presence. At the salon musical, Harrison Brand kept her close company and a parade of other eager young men did the same at every affair. The Monday evening with Craig was again thoroughly enjoyable, and though she felt that making comparisons was a particularly invidious habit, she found herself doing just that. Craig Emlyn more than held his own. She did not include Dean Fowler in her comparisons. She didn't even want to think about him though that continued to be a more difficult resolution to keep.

Yet the surface quality of the evenings made her seek mornings alone. More and more, she felt the need to let the morning's cool solitude wash over her and she began taking early rides on one of the carriage horses. The long, easy gallops across the plains was one thing she missed about Australia. Millicent rode away from Dean Fowler's property line and found a stand of woods that opened onto a series of mist-shrouded glens on the other side, each filled with purple gorse, bracken, and heather, a soft fire amid the mat of green moss and willows. It was a sun-speckled morning and she was trotting slowly through a narrow vale when Dean Fowler's big gray stallion appeared in her path.

She came to a halt as Dean Fowler himself nodded to her, his intense face unsmiling, his eyes taking in the soft cream of her skin, the vibrant beauty of her. She stared back with cool eyes until he finally spoke, the words tight, almost bitter. "I wondered how long it would take someone to discover these little glens of mine," he said.

"Little glens of yours?" Millicent echoed, her brows arching. "Do you lay claim to everything that's about? Is that a habit of yours?"

The bitterness of his tone grew a fraction rueful. "No, there are no claims here except ones of the heart," he said. His eyes met hers, a cool amusement sliding into them. "I see that the sharp edge of your tongue hasn't been dulled by your socializing," he remarked.

"Are you keeping watch on me, on my life?" Millicent asked.

"Hardly," he snapped. "But I do get about some and I hear talk. I also saw your name in the social columns of the *Times*. The beautiful Lady Millicent and yet another escort, I believe it said."

Millicent acknowledged the quotation with a slight nod. "Is there something wrong with that?" she slid out.

Dean Fowler shrugged. "Trying to prove something?" he returned.

Millicent felt her lips tighten. "This conversation is at an end," she bit out. Angry, she brought her hand down hard on the horse's rump, a sharp, smart

155

slap. Entirely unprepared for his instant reaction, she almost fell as the horse half-rose, and leaped forward into a full gallop. She tried to rein up but he was almost full out. She saw the moss-covered log and felt the horse ignore her pull on the reins. He went into the jump before she was ready and she felt herself lose her seat. Flinging her arms out for balance, she tried to cling to his back but it was impossible. She felt herself sailing through the air, and heard a half-scream coming from her own lips. All she could think of was that she must miss hitting the log. She wrapped her arms tightly around herself, and hit the ground only inches from the log. She landed on her left side, her shoulder striking first, then her head. The ground was moss-covered, but shock exploded through her body and the tree branches above her seemed suddenly on a carousel as the world started to spin. A soft, fuzzy curtain of gray descended over her eyes.

She lay still, dimly conscious of her own breathing, aware of pain. She felt a hand circling the back of her neck, and opened her eyes. The gray curtain was still there and she shook her head to make the curtain lift. She started to pull herself up on one elbow, and slowly brought her eyes into focus. A strong, handsome face came into view, concern stark in the blue eyes as she pulled her self up to a sitting position. She managed a rueful smile and winced. "I'm all right," she said. Dean Fowler's hand moved from the back of her neck and supported her as she sat, drawing a deep breath. "My fault. He's a former drum horse of the Royal Irish Hussars. I should have known he'd respond like that." She moved her shoulder and winced again. "Just a bruise," she said.

"Probably," he replied, "but let's be sure." His hands moved over her shoulder, along the back of her neck, then down her back, moving her arm, strong hands yet surprisingly gentle. They moved down her arms, pressing gently at the joints, then along the top of her legs. She felt the warmth of his touch through the riding skirt exceedingly pleasant and she lay back, letting him finish. "Nothing broken," he said, finally. "Just a sprain or two. You took a good fly from the saddle."

He pulled her back to a sitting position, his face only inches from hers. She looked up into the intenseness of his eyes and suddenly the moment was charged with electricity. Millicent felt her lips part and then his mouth was upon hers, pressing, hungering. Her arms lifted, slid around his shoulders, and she ignored the pain in her left shoulder. She felt surprise at his boldness but more at the surge of her own desire. Slowly, he drew back, and peered deep into her eyes, a touch of imperiousness in his face again.

"I trust that wasn't too coldly detached for you," he said quietly.

"No, not at all," she murmured. Slowly, she brought her arms down.

"I've been wanting to do that ever since I met

157

you," he said. She held back the reply that came to her lips, the revelation that she had wanted the same. The intensity of the thought took her by surprise. He moved to sit down beside her on the elf-cup moss. "That evening we spent together is all I think about," he said.

"I think of it, too," Millicent admitted. His hand reached out to take hers, enfolding her delicate fingers entirely.

"Look here, I know I tore things up rather badly but I want to change that," he said. "I want to see you again, as often as possible. I don't want our disagreements to stand between us."

"I'm rather afraid they do," Millicent said.

"They needn't," Dean told her. "We disagree on the right thing to do regarding Sir Thomas's letter so we'll just put it aside for now. We'll forget about it. I don't want that to stop you from seeing me."

Millicent met his eyes, noticing the strong seriousness of his face. She wanted to cry out agreement, wanted terribly to believe his words, yet the question stabbed at her, demanded to be given voice. "How do I know this isn't simply a campaign to make me feel differently, to soften my attitude?" she asked. "How can I know this isn't just another way to get Haddington Hall?"

His eyes didn't leave hers. "You can't know," he said gravely. "You will have to take my word that it's not."

"That's honest," Millicent said. "And if I do not take your word?"

"I'll be most unhappy," Dean said softly.

"I want to believe you," Millicent said, trying to probe behind his brilliant blue eyes.

His answer was to lean forward and press his lips to hers again. "Will this help?" he murmured. She drank of his kiss until he drew away, his hand held against her cheek.

"Yes," she murmured. The touch of his lips was indeed a message. Wanting might only be desire but there had been tenderness in his lips as well. Deceit could hide in wanting. Tenderness allowed room only for honesty.

"A new beginning," he said as he rose, and lifted her to her feet. The bruises didn't hurt at all, now, she noted. She waited as he returned her horse, which had halted a dozen yards away. His hands on her waist as she mounted brought soft strength, comforting warmth. "Will you be able to ride back?" he asked with a concerned frown.

"Quite well," she said. "I'll go slowly."

"When will you have dinner with me?" he asked, his hand over hers on the cantle. Mentally, she raced through her catalog of engagements, and crossed out one.

"Thursday?" she answered

"Thursday it is," he said. "Will you be riding here tomorrow morning?" She nodded and his smile curled around her. "We shall ride together, then," he said. "Now go home and fetch yourself some liniment."

She turned the horse and went off, not looking back, afraid that if she did, she'd not leave. But she felt his eyes following her and when she returned to Haddington Hall, she had Rupert stable the horse. Sarah was there as she entered.

"Fetch me something for sprains and bruises, please," Millicent said.

"Not bruises of the spirit," Sarah commented. "You're fairly glowing."

"How true, only bruises of the body," Millicent laughed. "I'll tell you all about it when you come upstairs."

Millicent found the aches quickly making themselves felt as she climbed the stairway. In her room, she undressed to a petticoat, and lay across the bed. Sarah arrived soon after, the bottle in one hand, a stack of cloths in the other. She sat down on the edge of the bed, and unstoppered the bottle. Millicent inhaled the slightly sharp odor. "My own root liniment," Sarah said as she began to rub it over the bruised left shoulder. "comfrey root, columbine root, boiling water, and a bit of wormwood oil," Sarah said. The ointment felt soothingly warm, Millicent's skin drinking it in, as she recounted the events of the morning, leaving out nothing. She finished at almost the same moment Sarah ended the massage. Millicent turned on her side, and scanned Sarah's face, suddenly impassive.

"What is it?" she asked, picking up signals. "I believe Dean."

"That's obvious," the older woman said.

Millicent's lips turned into a half-pout. "And you don't think I should?"

"I didn't say that," Sarah answered, letting a small sigh escape her. "It's that you're plainly taken with this man and I don't want to see you hurt. Perhaps he is everything you want. Perhaps you can believe him. But not so fast. You should continue as you have been, seeing others, enjoying life, especially with Craig Emlyn. You've said you find him attractive, too."

"Yes," Millicent admitted.

"It's far too early for burning bridges, that's what I'm saying. Wait and see," Sarah cautioned. "Wait till you can be certain of what you want to believe. And of yourself."

Millicent nodded, sat up, and hugged the ample form. Sarah's advice was good, as always. "Agreed. No burning bridges until I'm sure," she said. Satisfied, Sarah's round face settled back into its usual pleasantness, and she hurried from the room. Millicent rested, took a hot bath later, and went to bed early to hasten the morning on its way.

She was up early, the sprains and bruises considerably better, though she wasn't sure which had done the most good, the liniment for the body or the liniment for the spirit. A heavy mist lay over the ground, turning the little glens into fairyland spots. When she

161

reached the second of the glens, the gray stallion rose up from the mists as though he had no legs and were a floating steed.

"The mists become you," Dean said. "A cape of delicacy for the princess of the glens." He reached out, and took her hand as he swung the stallion in beside her horse. They rode slowly through the silent mists, watching the strands shred and come together again to form new wispy scarves. There seemed no need for idle talk, no need to make conversation. She felt warmly comfortable beside this strong-faced man, almost as though she had known him for years. When the sun came to burn away the mist, they found a flat rock and rested upon it. Only once did his lips find hers, briefly, a clinging moment, the tenderness there again and Millicent was sorry to see time hurry the day on.

The morning set a pattern, one that became a daily routine. She looked forward to the soft beginnings that marked each day. They talked of many things. To rest in his arms seemed as natural as breathing. She learned of the depth of his breeding program and his hopes and aims made themselves known, as different sides of him took on form and substance for her. She actually saw Dean only infrequently in the evenings. There were mares to foal, stock to see to, chores that needed doing, all the time-consuming part of running a breeding farm. But the early mornings became theirs and she'd not exchange one for all the evenings of fun and parties.

But Dean was not the only pattern that developed. Craig was at almost every one of the affairs she attended, sometimes just meeting her there, more often as her escort. He had his own weapons; his boyish charm, his effortless wit, a touch of wildness. Dean made her feel warm, stirring deep and throbbing needs with his every glance, every touch of his lips. Craig made her sparkle and glisten and feel a heady touch of wantonness and delightfully wicked. Dean was fine, rich sherry, Craig bubbling champagne and the others *vin ordinaire*. It had come down to that and she confided as much to the Countess de Berrie during an affair they both attended.

"How exciting," the woman said, her eyes gleaming. "Just continue to keep me informed. And drink up," she added. "I envy you with two such handsome choices. I'd prefer the champagne, of course."

"We shall see," Millicent laughed, but remembered the Countess's words in the busy, crowded weeks that followed. She was surprised herself at how much she did enjoy Craig's company while, when she was with Dean, there seemed nothing for her but his quiet intenseness. Her lips responded to his as they did for no one else, and the times with him were more than passing pleasure. It was, she decided, her sense of fairness, not fickleness, that delayed her decision. The meeting with Craig's family, which she could no longer find an excuse to put off, took place on a Sunday afternoon for high tea.

Lord and Lady Emlyn's large, austere house was

surrounded by what seemed acres upon acres of pink peonies and trillium. The flowers formed an inviting vista, soft and appealing, but they did little to offset the character of Lord and Lady Emlyn. His Lordship, a tall man with a clipped mustache, the sand color of Craig's hair but duller, greeted Millicent first as Craig brought her into the house. He moved with a stiff, mechanical gait, and sat as stiffly as he stood and Millicent wondered if he could bend at all, physically or emotionally. Lady Emlyn was fashioned out of the same mold, a tall woman dressed in a severe white gown, with silvered hair and light-blue eyes. Lady Emlyn smiled often but the smile was as mechanical as a metal pull-toy. Bloodless people, Millicent found herself thinking and wondered where Craig had inherited his charm. A grandparent, no doubt, she decided.

"Craig has told us so much about you, my dear," Lady Emlyn said, making it sound as though she wished he hadn't.

"He's quite fond of you," Lord Emlyn growled through his bristly mustache.

"I'm very fond of Craig," Millicent answered. His Lordship left most of the conversational gambits to Lady Emlyn and the woman kept up a casual flow of small talk as tea was served. The social whirl, mutual acquaintances, the state of her gardens, everything flowed smoothly and it wasn't till the afternoon was half-over that Millicent became aware of the questions that Lady Emlyn slipped into the conversation, questions that touched, almost oddly, on her family history, Sir Thomas's lineage and background. Suddenly Millicent realized that she was being interrogated, most cleverly, yet nonetheless interrogated. She became cautious with her answers, alert to casual queries, and she felt a stab of resentment. She would have much preferred direct, open questions. The method of inquiry had had an air of subterfuge about it, not at all redeemed by a genteel veneer, and Millicent was glad when the afternoon came to an end.

Craig took her home and seemed totally unaware of the undercurrents of the visit. "I know they liked you," he told her. "I can tell." Perhaps he could, Millicent reflected as he went on happily bubbling over the afternoon. She kissed Craig, feeling curiously uncaring, and went into Haddington Hall with a tiny frown in the center of her forehead. But the real proof, which had lain all along in the quiet places of the heart, came to her in a reverse sort of way. Craig had to go to Birmingham on business with Lord Emlyn and was gone for most of an entire week. Millicent missed his presence at two affairs that he would have made infinitely less boring, but it was in the way one misses a coat one has grown used to wearing. The very next week Dean had to spend five days in Yorkshire and suddenly the world was an empty place, the mornings desolate, his absence a void that made her ache. She found herself counting the days, wrapped in anxious hours, waiting for the moment when she would again see the gray stallion appear through the early dawn mists. She shared the realization with Sarah over a cup of late night tea in the silence of the great house.

"It is indeed a strange world, you know?" Millicent thought aloud between sips. "Some things don't come to us straight-out at all. They slip in through the back door, as it were, and we don't really *decide* anything about how we feel. I mean there's no reasoned, rational decision at all. Suddenly everything is just what it is, decided for us, all made of things we can't explain but are simply there."

"What is it you're trying to tell me?" Sarah asked patiently.

"I rather guess I'm trying to tell you that I'm terribly in love with Dean," Millicent answered slowly, turning the sound of the words over inside her as she said them, liking the sweet sound of them.

"I imagined you'd settle on him," Sarah murmured.

"He's everything I want, Sarah," Millicent said.

"And his feelings toward you?"

"I know he cares very much."

"Has he mentioned marriage?" Sarah asked.

"Not yet, but I'm certain he will," Millicent said.

"And Haddington Hall? You're still certain his feelings toward you have nothing to do with the house and land?" Sarah pressed.

"Absolutely certain," Millicent said quickly. "I just know it."

"How do you just know it?" Sarah insisted.

"There are ways to tell such things," Millicent returned.

"Yes, there are, I'll admit that," Sarah agreed. "And there are also ways to let yourself think what you want to think."

"You're too cynical", Millicent protested.

Sarah reached out, and pressed her hand. "No, my dear. I don't mean to be that. I hope you're right. I want you to be right. I just don't want to see you hurt."

"I won't be," Millicent assured her. "My bold venture has succeeded, Sarah, beyond my fondest expectations. I've no need to seek further. I need only to wait a little longer, now."

"And Craig? You'll stop seeing him, now?"

"Not at once. There are too many engagements where it's expected I'll be with him. It would be embarrassing for him to suddenly seem discarded, like an old shoe. I wouldn't do that to Craig. He's been much too sweet."

"What will you do, then?"

"Go to all the engagements already on my list with him and then, in my own way, taper off gradually so that he won't suddenly appear in the role of the jilted suitor," Millicent said.

"I expect he'll be in that role no matter how nicely you do it," Sarah commented.

"Perhaps, but it needn't be done in the cruelest way," Millicent said and meant every word. There was no excuse to make Craig a victim of all the social gossip that would follow a sudden jilting. Her decision also made her feel less guilty at having offered Craig such encouragement as she had when, deep inside her, she had longed for Dean from the very first. Later, alone in her spacious bed, she reflected on all the other words that she wanted to say now that she had faced her true feelings. No schoolgirl infatuation this, and no sliding into an expected marriage, as it had been with Jock. Love, in all its deep and throbbing sorcery, had taken hold of her. For the very first time, Millicent reflected, life was everything it should be.

There would be no more games, not with Dean, she told herself. No more cautious phrases, no more careful honesty. She felt a tremendous sense of relief in escaping this world of pretenses that she had plunged into with such determination. In the one, all-important matter in her life, she would indulge in no more of that. There was no need any longer, and she smiled in the darkness of her room. Love should never involve deceit and pretense. She slept, finally, happier than she had ever been before. Bold ventures can bring bold loves.

The moment to turn words into reality came at the end of the week, on a cloudless morning amid the purple gorse of the glens. Dean waited beside her horse, and lifted her to the ground as she came to a halt. "I missed you terribly," she said at once, her eyes grave even as his strong arms pulled her to him. She waited, a split-second of fear flashing inside her.

"No more than I missed you, my Millicent," he said. "That would be impossible." His lips found hers, sweet strength, and his words circled inside her, more than words she wanted to hear but an exchange of honesty, a meeting of hearts. She returned his kisses, sank down on the soft moss-covered ground beside him, and drew the comfort and strength of his arms around her. Then she listened as he spoke of the week away from her.

"Except for thinking about you constantly, it was a good trip," Dean said. "I picked up a line of fine stock that will be sent by next week." He turned her in his arms to face him, his eyes peering deeply into hers. "And I learned a lot of new information on the latest breeding theories and picked up a good bit of practical information. But I learned one thing more, of greater importance than anything else. I learned how much I love you."

His lips pressed down onto hers, his words throbbing inside her, warm, wonderful, words that would forever tick away in the depths of her heart. "I didn't go anywhere but I also learned how much I care, my darling," Millicent said and wondered if he could hear the pounding in her chest as he held her close. Finally he drew back, his eyes searching hers again.

"I had to tell you that, first," he said. "Before I ask a favor of you."

"You needn't ask. Any favor I can grant is yours," Millicent said.

"No, I must ask," Dean told her. "You know that I've not so much as breathed a word about Haddington Hall. I've not allowed it to intrude in any way between us."

"Indeed, you have kept that promise," Millicent nodded.

"I still want it that way," Dean said. "But this large shipment of stock—mares, some close to foaling, stallions, young colts—will be more than I can stable on my land, I realize now. You have three large, fine stables standing empty. I ask use of them until I can build additions to my own."

"They are yours, my love," Millicent answered at once.

Dean's hands held her shoulders, their warm strength flowing through her. "Some people will say that I soft-talked you into this. Only you and I will know differently," he cautioned.

"Let them think whatever they will," Millicent said.

"Then it's agreed. I'll be asking a very special question of you soon, anyway, my love," Dean said. "But a man must have all his affairs in order before that question is broached."

He drew her to him again. *A special question,* Millicent repeated silently to herself. There was but one special question, of course, and the very thought curled inside her like a Cheshire cat. He could ask it now so far as she was concerned. Her answer was ready, like an actor waiting in the wings to rush onstage. But she would wait, and savor every moment of the waiting.

Two evenings later, at an affair given by Lord Aylsworth which she was attending with Craig, she managed to take the Countess de Berrie aside for a private moment. "I'd say the Yorkshireman is winning," she confided to the woman.

The Countess responded to the tidbit the way a gambler responds to a gaming table, with instant excitement. "But you're here with Craig Emlyn," the Countess said.

"No matter, it's Dean Fowler," Millicent whispered.

The Countess wrapped herself in mischievous delight. "How absolutely wonderful. Everyone's saying it will be Craig Emlyn, he's with you so much." She made a happy little clicking sound with her mouth, her eyes dancing with amusement. "Now I can look terribly wise when the subject comes up. It will drive them to distraction wondering what I know that they don't. You're a perfect dear. I'll just love every minute of tomorrow's afternoon tea at Grace Magnussen's."

The Countess patted her arm, flashed a wide smile, and went sailing off in a cloud of velvet. Promises kept, Millicent smiled to herself. Besides, she had come to enjoy the Countess and her shallow preoccupations. It was fun secretly aiding her in keeping her position as high priestess of London society.

Millicent had told Sarah of Dean's request, of course, and also of what else he had said to her. "I'd have to say you are doing the right thing," Sarah said.

"Of course," Millicent returned. There'd never been the slightest doubt in her mind about that. She had acted as an understanding neighbor, not as a woman totally and completely in love. Dean wanted her to keep those aspects of herself apart and she could do so, Millicent told herself. She'd continue to do so until there was no longer any need, until he asked that special question. Time wasn't important any longer, just the inner knowledge that had given her wings of utter happiness.

CHAPTER EIGHT

Dean's new stock arrived a few days later and Millicent watched as he and two of his men drove the horses into the Haddington Hall stables. She caught Dean's wave, blew him a quick kiss, and saw the flash of his smile. The days passed on soft clouds; the only nettle to mar her happiness was the need to find a way to tell Craig of her feelings without hurting him too much. He was especially attentive at one of the three last events they'd planned together and she felt increasingly sorry for him. She'd begin the tapering off process as soon as the last affair was over, she vowed.

But a week later, in Dean's arms beneath a low-hanging willow in the morning sun, she saw troubled tightness in his face. "Something is disturbing you," she said. "What is it?"

He laughed with a touch of ruefulness. "You've come to know me too well," he said.

"That will never be," she answered. "What's troubling you? It's not my still going to affairs with Craig, is it? I explained to you that I don't want to hurt him abruptly."

"No, it's not that," he replied with a smile. "I understand that and admire your compassion."

It was a compliment but Millicent was suddenly not certain that she wouldn't have preferred a touch less understanding. "Then what is it, love?" she asked again.

His eyes were deep, filled with seriousness. "It's that I must ask your help again, my dear," he told her. "I need to build a half-dozen corrals running back from your stables. The stock I have there needs more exercise than they're getting."

"Yes, I imagine they do," Millicent said. "Then build your corrals, by all means."

His hands held her shoulders. "I don't want to intrude again on our bargain by mentioning Haddington Hall," he said. "It troubles me."

She rested a finger against his lips. "You concern yourself too much over a promise, a bargain that is no longer at all important."

He reflected for a moment, his eyes studying her. "Perhaps," he said, then, letting his hands move down to touch the sweet softness of her arm. "It will indeed be unimportant soon, when you are all mine."

His kiss stayed on her lips through the remainder of the day and later that evening Sarah, watching Millicent in the study, smiled gently at her. "I've never seen you so happy," the older woman remarked.

"That's because I've never been so happy," Millicent said. "When I marry Dean, you'll stay on, of course, won't you?" The thought had never made itself felt before and Millicent was suddenly assaulted by the implications. "I mean, you just have to, Sarah," she said, suddenly full of concern.

"We shall see," Sarah answered softly. "Decisions, then, won't be yours alone to make."

"That one will be," Millicent said sternly.

"Let's not put carts before the horses," Sarah admonished. "He hasn't asked you to marry him yet."

"Soon, though," Millicent said happily. "Almost every day he says something that edges around it."

Once again Millicent told herself that time was unimportant, now. During the following week, Dean's workmen constructed the corrals stretching behind the stables and by the end of the week the colts and mares were running freely about inside their new confines.

A few evenings later, she attended the last of the events she and Craig had planned together. She had avoided making any further commitments to him and was running out of excuses. She would soon have to tell Craig of her decision. But not this night. This was an evening he had looked forward to with special enthusiasm and she hadn't the heart to fling a shadow over the close of it. The occasion was a special lady's night at Boodle's, a very special evening sponsored and put on by the younger members of the club.

And it did indeed become a very convivial affair, where the champagne flowed freely and a festive air prevailed, with a certain bonhomie all too absent at many affairs. It was also a somewhat younger crowd than at many other gatherings, though the Countess de Berrie did put in an appearance to steal the spotlight from all the younger women. Near the evening's close, when sobriety had become a rare state, Craig left Millicent's side to see to a friend who had imbibed neither wisely nor well. She seated herself on a small settee near the open door of an adjoining smoking room when the voices came clearly to her. She recognized Reggie Van Alstine's voice first, then Peter Humphreys', Robert Asquith, and a young man she couldn't place. The quartet was in high spirits, more than a little raucous, she realized.

"I'd say you've lost your wager with Fowler, Peter," Millicent heard Reggie cry out.

"Not yet, old boy. He hasn't got Haddington Hall, yet," Millicent heard Peter Humphreys answer. She felt the frown dig into her forehead at once and her hand suddenly held tightly to the edge of the settee. *Leave*, a little voice told her, *leave at once*. But the other voices came booming from the room again, invisible chains that kept her in place.

"Oh, come, now," Reggie Van Alstine's voice said. "He's got her eating out of his hand. He's got his new stock quartered at her old stables and he's built new corrals on her land."

"That's not exactly winning our wager," Millicent heard Peter Humphreys protest and listened to the roar of derision that followed.

"Dean wagered you he'd have Haddington Hall one way or another, a hundred pounds it was, and I'd say he's got it," Reggie roared and the others joined in his laughter.

"I wonder if he had to promise to marry the beautiful Lady Millicent," one of the others said and another roar of laughter followed.

"I don't think he'd go that far," Peter Humphreys boomed. "Not old Dean. He'll get Haddington Hall on his own terms."

"Well, she is a beautiful package. Wouldn't mind giving that a bit of romancing, myself," the other voice chimed in and another gale of laughter resounded from the room. Millicent felt a nail break as her hands dug into the side of the settee. Her stomach had become a knot and a wave of nausea swept over her. She hadn't heard the words, she told herself. It was all a terrible dream, a nightmare. But the voices refused to stop, giving the lie to her wish, enforcing the horrible reality of it. "Well, he's not got it yet and I'm holding onto my hundred pounds until he does," Peter Humphreys said.

"Time, that's all old Dean needs, time," Reggie's voice answered and Millicent heard the clink of glasses raised in a toast. "Let's get a bit of air," someone else said and Millicent heard movement mingling with more ribald remarks, the sound of their voices suddenly turning toward the open door. They were leaving the room, coming her way. Panic swept over her and she wanted to run, to hide, but there was neither the time nor the place to do either. She forced her stomach to stop turning over and rose, unclenching her hands. There was no time to sort out her feelings, no time to even face the turmoil inside herself. But something gathered itself together, and rose out of the still unformed depths of her anguish, something born of betrayal not yet absorbed, rage not yet given purpose. Pride, perhaps, the sharp edge of self-respect, something that flooded through her, and made her turn to the doorway as she rose, her face carefully composed, an icy coolness in her eyes.

Reggie emerged first, and saw her, halted, then the others followed, their eyes widening, embarrassment flooding their collective features. Peter Humphreys blinked, an attack of sudden sobriety seizing him. It was obvious that she had heard their remarks. Her brows lifted as she fastened the quartet with an icy smile. "Was there really a wager?" she asked softly, almost casually.

Reggie had the good taste to look excruciatingly uncomfortable. "Yes, there was a wager," he said, his voice hardly audible. He gestured to the fourth young man. "Tom here acted as witness to it and to the amount wagered."

"But it was all in fun," Peter Humphreys added hastily, apologetically.

Millicent's cold smile remained. "Yes, how amusing," she said, surprised at the calmness in her voice. "Particularly in view of the fact that wagers can be made by many people."

She saw them frown, and exchange quick glances. Then Reggie's eyes returned to her, fighting through a slightly alcoholic fog. "Are you saying that someone else wagered on that?" he slurred.

"You shouldn't assume that wagering on such matters is a male prerogative," Millicent slid out.

Reggie's mouth fell open for a moment, then, his face gathering astonishment, he took the bait she had tossed out. "You mean it's been a turn-about all along?" he breathed. "You've wagered on old Dean making his move. Good God, that's rich."

"I shan't say anything more on the matter, gentlemen," Millicent returned loftily, spinning on her heel and walking away, her head held high.

"You might still win that hundred pounds, Peter," she heard Robert Asquith say excitedly. They'd discuss the turn among themselves for days, perhaps eventually deciding they'd never determine the details. But they'd stop seeing her as a dupe, a laughingstock. It was a minor victory, perhaps, yet the only one left her. She sought out Craig, keeping her face a mask. The mask had to stay on a little longer, just long enough to get her home.

"I've grown quite tired," she told Craig when she found him. "I really should like to go home before I collapse."

Craig was instantly solicitous, getting her cape and calling for his carriage at once. She was happy to let him ramble on about the evening as the carriage made its way back to Haddington Hall. She needed but to intersperse a comment here and there. Witty as he was, quick with a quip and so very attentive, Craig was not really perceptive and she found herself grateful for that. *Small favors accepted,* she murmured silently. He hadn't picked up her churning tensions at all, his voice droning on as her hands clenched and unclenched. The mask was slipping away and she closed her eyes for a moment and forced herself not to think of words that refused to stop whirling inside her. She opened her eyes, and saw Haddington Hall come into view, rising up darkly under a moonless sky. She was trembling when the carriage came to a halt outside the door, and started to leave at once, but Craig's hand on her arm stopped her. She saw a spark of uncertainty begin in his eyes.

"Something wrong?" he asked tentatively.

"I'm simply exhausted," she said. "Forgive me, darling." The mask had to stay on a few moments longer. "It was a lovely evening, especially memorable," she said, unable to keep the grimness from her voice. She waited as Craig's lips brushed her cheek.

"Yes, a fabulous evening, wasn't it?" he agreed. "Friday night?"

She nodded quickly as she stepped from the carriage. "Yes, Friday night," she said and saw his face brighten at once.

"Sleep well, love," he called after her as she turned, and almost ran into the house. The mask shredded, and her face broke into lines of drawn anguish. She raced up the dark stairway as great, gasping sobs began even before she reached her room. Once inside, she tore off her gown and flung herself across the bed. Shock swept over her in all its enormity, now, no need to fight to hold it back, searing, consuming, shattering in its immensity. She had so believed in Dean, had been so certain she had found love in all its glorious happiness. All the unformed feelings that had swept over her in the club now began to take shape; anger, betrayal, pain, all gargoyles of the soul that grinned mockingly at her.

In but a few, brief moments, the overflowing heart had been emptied, like a goblet knocked over, all its contents of happiness spilling out. Champagne had loosened tongues, raised voices in carelessness, and truth had been set free. *In vino veritas,* she sobbed. And in truth lay a terrible pain. The irony of it stabbed deep inside her. She had come here to enter this world of superficialities, planned and prepared, had mounted her own deceits so carefully, and then had cast it all aside because the heart makes its own rules. Sarah's words spun out of the dark at her. *You could be playing a dangerous game.* But it had ceased to be a game, not with Dean. She had followed her heart, as if she could have done anything else, she wondered. She had believed in Dean, in his strength, in the tenderness of his lips, and in his words. She had believed in his love.

Love. The word seemed suddenly drenched in bitterness. Betrayal, not love, had been his offering. The strong, handsome face materialized before her and inside her, it seemed a knife turned and twisted, cutting her into shreds. All the words, all the sweet moments, the touch of his hands, his lips, the comfort of his arms, were all now hollow, just as she was now hollow, emptied, a creature made of dull and aching voids.

She lay awake most of the night. Sleep was as fitful as a summer breeze, coming only in brief moments that drifted into wakefulness moments later. Slowly cold rage gathered itself, the fury of betrayal rising up inside her. She watched the dawning of the day, rose, and slowly dressed in her riding outfit. She would shed no more tears, not from a shriveled heart. She saddled her horse as the morning mists swirled. Seething rage was her shield, now, her armor the steel of the wounded heart, her banner the cross of betrayal. She rode out into the morning carrying the night behind her.

She was at the glen first, already waiting when the

gray stallion appeared. She dismounted, her knuckles white around the riding crop. Dean rode up and swung to the ground, his tall, strong figure starting toward her. She saw a tiny furrow touch his brow as he sensed something at once. Millicent felt a terrible desire to rush into his arms, to feel his lips on hers. Even shattered, the heart had its habits.

"Good morning, love," he said, reaching for her.

Millicent stepped backward. "You may stop pretending," she snapped. "The game is over."

Dean's frown deepened as he halted, his brilliant blue eyes peering at her. "What are you talking about?" he asked.

"A hundred pounds," she bit out. She took satisfaction in seeing surprise leap into his face. "That is one of the risks in being a wagering man. One loses sometimes."

Dean's eyes narrowed. "How did you hear about that?" he asked.

"A chance accident. A bit of good fortune, shall we say? For me, that is."

"Look here, it's not the way it sounds," he began.

"Isn't it?" she cut him off. "No, I'd say it was far worse than it sounds."

"No, listen to me," he said.

"A hundred pounds you'd have Haddington Hall one way or another," she said icily. "Are you denying you made that wager?" She fastened a stare of cold fury on him while suddenly hoping he would deny it, somehow sweep away everything she had

183

heard in one grand gesture, even the witness to the wager. But that was only hope giving one last, impossible gasp, she realized.

Dean's lips tightened, hardly moving as he answered. "No, there was a wager. I can't deny that. But I can explain it," he said.

"Explain it? No doubt you can find a way to do that. You're very clever with words. You know how to wield them with such sweet reason and how to wrap promises in their veils," Millicent said, her voice close to breaking. "You must have enjoyed telling your friends how easily you were winning your wager."

"I didn't do anything of the kind," he protested.

"But you didn't call off the wager, did you?" she snapped back.

He looked unhappy as he gave a half-shrug. "I didn't think about doing so. It was unimportant," he said.

"A hundred pounds, a wager important enough to make but not to call off?" she speared. "I'm not that much a fool."

"But it was unimportant. You don't understand," he said.

He was trying to placate her, the handsome, strong man she loved trying to calm her as though she were an upset child. Her love crystallized into hate and erupted in all its fury.

"Understand?" she cried. "I understand for the first time. I was such a willing dupe. I believed everything you said, all the sweet words, the loving words, and the very first promise you made about Haddington Hall. And then, after you'd had me in the palm of your hand, you reluctantly asked about using the stables. You were so sweetly unhappy about that, then the corrals. How upset you were at having to ask me. Oh, you did it all so well."

"Stop it!" Dean thundered. "Listen to me. Let me explain."

"Listen to more lies? Oh, no, I've listened enough. I'll never believe another word you say. That's something you can wager upon," she flung back. He reached out for her, his hand grasping her arm, anger in his face.

"No, damn you, you'll listen," he said. Millicent brought her riding crop up in a short arc, and twisted away from his grip as she brought it down. He ducked, but not fast enough and the crop seared a thin line of red along his temple.

"Stay away from me!" she almost screamed. "Clear your stock from my stables today and take down your corrals or I shall call the sheriff."

She swung onto her horse as Dean, touching the line of red on his temple, stared at her, his face drawn, his mouth a thin line. "I'll talk to you when your hysterics have ended," he said with quiet anger.

She glared down from the saddle. "My hysterics may end. The hurting will never end," she said, wheeling the horse in a tight circle and galloping away before he could see the tears welling up in her eyes. It takes time to stop loving, she had once heard, and understood that now. But she'd let rage and fury be her allies. Most of all, she'd not let herself ever give her heart again. Giving only left one vulnerable, especially in this world of pretenses and games. She galloped back to the house, gave the horse to Rupert, and hurried inside. Sarah was there as she entered, and saw the tearstains still streaking her face. Millicent beckoned her into the study, closed the door, and poured out everything between sobs and moments of cold rage, starting with those horrible moments at the club. She sank down onto the edge of a straight-backed chair as she finished, trembling, her face drawn tightly.

"I'm so sorry, my dear," Sarah said. "And surprised. I didn't take the gentleman as being that callous."

"I was wrong about him. His selfish, callous cleverness is just another part of his arrogance," Millicent answered.

"Perhaps you should have heard him out," Sarah suggested.

"Why? To hear more lies, more smooth, clever explanations?" Millicent threw back. "He didn't deny the wager. Of course, he couldn't very well, not with a witness involved in the entire shoddy business. And he had to admit he'd done nothing to retract the wager. No, I shall never listen to anything he has to say again."

186

"What will you do, now?" Sarah asked. "Perhaps it's too soon to answer that."

"Not at all," Millicent snapped, lifting her chin. "I shall go on as if I'd never met Dean Fowler. He shall simply cease to exist for me." She saw the doubt in Sarah's eyes. "That's right," Millicent insisted. "He'll be a cipher. Just give me a little while and I shall hardly remember his name." Sarah still looked doubtful. "You'll see," Millicent said. "I shall start by accepting all those invitations I had set aside to turn down. And there's no reason not to see Craig even more, now."

"No reason at all," Sarah said quietly and Millicent ignored the unspoken criticism in the reply. Sarah left her as she attacked the bowl of unanswered invitations and announcements. It was a new beginning, a renewed plunge into the mainstream of London society and she sent off acceptances with grim vengeance, determined to fill every waking hour with festivity or fatigue. Either would do, so long as there was not a stray moment for Dean to creep into her thoughts. She would hurry time again, but differently, now.

She was in her room when Dean came the following day. She refused to see him, and let Sarah carry the refusal as she drew the curtains on the windows. As he rode away, she peered through a slit in the curtains, and watched his face set, his lips pressed tightly together. She forced the sob from her throat, flung it aside, and turned from the window to let love

187

twist itself into hate again. It wasn't all that difficult. She had only to think of how she had been nothing more than a pawn in a crude wager, played for a silly little fool. She kept the thought before her through the rest of the day, held onto it until night, when sleep came to rescue her.

She was downstairs with Sarah the next morning when a carriage arrived, the driver bearing a letter, a square, blue envelope, the initials DF engraved in darker blue on the reverse flap. "Shall I wait for an answer, ma'm?" the driver asked somewhat apprehensively, catching the ice in Millicent's face.

"I shall give it to you at once," Millicent said as she took the envelope, held it up, and tore it in two with a grand and satisfying flourish. She handed the two torn halves back to the startled carriageman. "Take it back to your employer," she bit out. "That is my answer."

The man half-bowed, then left in haste. Millicent felt Sarah's eyes watching her as she turned away and went up to her room. That evening she fled to a ball with Craig, danced to the very end, and on the carriage ride home she answered his lips as she never had before, sinking back into the soft, cushioned sides of the carriage with him. When they drew up before Haddington Hall and she opened the door of the carriage, she saw Craig looking at her with an expression not unlike someone who'd just been given an unexpected inheritance, a combination of surprise and pleasure not yet assimilated.

"That was a bit of all right," he breathed and Millicent patted his cheek, leaving him with the thought and hurrying into the house. In her room, she flung her clothes off and drew sleep around her at once. It was the first of a carousel of evenings where her beauty and wit found a new edge. Dean called at Haddington Hall twice, only to be turned away each time. Once, when Millicent was in the clarence, she saw him turn his horse to move toward her.

"Drive, as fast as you can," she called to Rupert, insisting he press the horses to reckless speeds. Looking back through the tiny rear window, she saw Dean halt his gray stallion after a few moments, obviously electing not to pursue her. She had made herself quite clear, she sniffed in satisfaction.

A few days later, at an afternoon social, she saw the Countess de Berrie and told her that it was now Craig who had her favors.

"Gracious, this changes flavor almost every week," the Countess observed. "But I love it. It lets me keep them all off balance."

"I doubt it shall change flavor again," Millicent said. "I'm finding Craig quite perfect."

"I'll wait for the next bulletin," the Countess said with a twinkle. "You're coming to my little affair next week, aren't you, my dear?" Millicent nodded at once. "Perhaps you can have something really exciting for me to spring on everyone. I should like that," the Countess added.

"I shall try," Millicent replied, although she did not yet have a plan. However, not twenty-four hours passed before she came to a decision, events coming together to trigger her into acting. The first was Sarah frowning over the ledger as Millicent, coming unexpectedly into the study, surprised her.

"Trouble?" Millicent asked at once, aware that she hadn't been paying enough attention to the state of the exchequer.

"Not quite yet," Sarah said, pursing her lips. "But pretty soon, I'm afraid. Time is running out, my dear." Millicent's brow knitted in a frown. "We never did have unlimited resources," Sarah reminded her. "We've done remarkably well in view of the cost of keeping up Haddington Hall."

"Keeping up my little charade, you mean," Millicent said, her voice tinged with sudden bitterness.

"Doing what you came here to do," Sarah corrected her sternly.

Millicent accepted the correction, met Sarah's gaze, and saw other thoughts held back. "Go on," she said. "Out with it, Sarah."

"Before time runs out, why not listen to Dean?" Sarah suggested.

Millicent felt anger spear at her instantly. "Listen to Dean? In heaven's name, why?" she snapped.

"Because you're still in love with him," Sarah said.

"Absolutely not," Millicent almost shouted. "He destroyed that completely. How could you even think such a thing?"

"I think you ought to at least hear what he has to say," Sarah said, ignoring the question.

"And be lied to again? Let myself believe him again, trust in him again? You ask me to open myself to more deceit, more being hurt?"

"I suppose I am, in a way. I'm really just suggesting you hear him out," Sarah answered.

"No, never. There's no point to it, Sarah," Millicent said. "I couldn't believe anything he said. I'd always wonder if it was all just more smooth words, more cleverness cloaked in some ulterior motive. I'd always wonder if there was another wager, perhaps one he'd made with himself for his own arrogant amusement. No, absolutely not. I'll listen to nothing from Mr. Dean Fowler."

Sarah regarded her thoughtfully, her eyes soft with sympathy. "I'm sorry you hurt so much, my dear," the older woman said.

"Hurt? Not anymore," Millicent answered haughtily. "I'm actually quite taken with Craig. I just never let myself see how sweet he is." Sarah didn't reply, but in her eyes Millicent saw the silent disbelief. "And time shan't run out, I promise," Millicent said.

Sarah accepted the remark with a nod and brought out a copy of the London *Times* with a section circled. "Something I thought you'd enjoy," she said, "as well as keep your days busy."

"So I don't think about Dean Fowler?" Millicent returned. "I assure you, I've stopped that."

"That's good," Sarah said blandly. "Then this can simply be something for you to enjoy."

Millicent took the newspaper, and peered at the item Sarah had circled.

ANNUAL FLOWER SHOW

The Greater London Flower Show will be held at Thornbury Hall as always. One of the most beautiful and popular events of the year, the annual Flower Show promises to attract even more entries than ever. The show is open to entrants who are residents of the greater London area.

The Board of Governors of the Royal Horticultural Society will judge all entries, choosing on a basis of design, color, beauty, and the quality of the flowers in the entry.

Miss Cynthia Wright of Paddington has been the Grand Prize Winner for the past two years.

"You always had such a wonderful way with flowers, even in that dustbin of a country, Australia," Sarah said as Millicent finished reading. "I think you ought to enter. You'd enjoy it so and it is the thing to do, you know."

Millicent's eyes took on a sparkle at once, the thought immensely appealing. "It would be fun," she mused aloud. "I know I'd love to prepare an absolutely smashing entry. Let me think a bit more about it."

"Not too long," Sarah warned. "You'll just have time to design and grow an entry as it is."

"I won't take too long," Millicent said and went up the wide stairs to prepare for the evening. The idea of working with flowers again filled her with anticipation, but she set aside thoughts about it for the moment, undressed to her petticoats, and rested until it was time to get ready for the evening. Craig was scheduled to arrive early and he would be prompt. Every word, every gesture, every implication had to be considered now. She had set her objective and now Craig was the key to it. She had already set all the peripheral wheels in motion. The time had come to send events hastening to their conclusion. Word had already reached her, in the roundabout, convoluted manner of such gossip in London social circles, that Cynthia Wright had been quick to try to step into the breach she had left with Dean. She remembered the girl well. She was too sweet, with a falseness inside her masked by a deceptively pretty face. Millicent felt her lips grow tight. If Dean thought to make her jealous, with Cynthia Wright, he would find that little gambit turning in on himself. She would not only show him she wasn't the least bit jealous but also that she had ceased to think about him, her needs quite well fulfilled.

He could well sit upon his arbitrary demands for Haddington House and glower across the land at her with Cynthia Wright beside him. She finished dressing, putting on a gown with echoes of the *troubadour* style Ingres favored in his paintings of prominent women. Craig was indeed prompt as always, and she settled back in his carriage as they made their way to the Duke of Chichester's town house.

Craig seemed especially ebullient. Though he tried to appear matter-of-fact, the words almost tumbled from him. "I've been hearing some most pleasant gossip," he remarked and Millicent let her eyebrows lift just a fraction in a mildly questioning glance. "Indeed," Craig went on, "I've heard it is being said in certain circles that the lovely Lady Millicent is favoring a certain Craig Emlyn."

Millicent let her laugh tinkle lightly. "The Countess de Berrie," she said. "You always were her favorite. She's whispered confidences to you. Shameful," Millicent said with mock severity.

Craig took her hands in his, his face suddenly wreathed in earnestness. "Then it's true?" he asked.

Millicent felt herself hesitate and a stab of fright went through her at the pause. She heard the answer rushing from her, swept from her lest she hesitate again, lest something or someone interfere with her determination. "Of course, it's true," she said. "It's absolutely true."

Craig's eyes widened, the boyish charm virtually exploding in his face as he pulled her to him. "By God, Millicent, I can't put off saying it any longer. I want to marry you," he blurted out. Millicent pulled back from his embrace to study him for a long moment, taking in the wide-eyed eagerness, his unique combination of sophistication and naiveté. He wasn't arrogant enough to disguise emotions or strong enough to hide deceit, and she was grateful for that. "Well, my darling? Will you marry me?" Craig asked excitedly.

Millicent felt that her smile was touched with a hint of rue, and broadened it at once to become warm and excited. Wings weren't all that important, she heard a tiny voice say inside herself. Love was made of pain. She had found that out. "Yes," she said simply, the single word suddenly quite all she could muster. He pulled her to him again and held her so tightly she could hardly breathe. "But I want the Countess to announce the engagement," she said, pulling back. "She'll enjoy that so much."

"Yes, won't she," Craig said, growing sober at once. "But the family ought to do it, you know." He frowned.

Millicent's mind raced. The Countess had been promised and the Countess had become an important friend. One had to think of importances in this social strata. "They can make the formal announcement," Millicent said brightly. "The Countess can do her own, informal one."

"Splendid," Craig said, slapping his knee. "I just hope I can keep quiet about it until next week."

He pulled her to him again, pressed his lips to hers until she begged for time to breathe. The excitement of it all made him not only terribly happy but also saw him at his most exuberantly witty during the rest of the evening. Millicent was pleased at how contained she felt about the turn of events. Excitement, longing, wild happiness, those were schoolgirl emotions. A pleasant satisfaction was sufficient, she told herself. On the ride home, she found herself restraining Craig's attempts for more kisses than she deemed proper.

"We are engaged, not married," she reminded him with some asperity. He accepted the admonition with a hint of petulance but took himself in rein. Haddington Hall was still and dark when she arrived there, everyone asleep, and she was glad for that. She had decided not to tell Sarah anything until after the Countess's party and didn't permit herself to wonder why.

She slept at once, not at all soundly, finally overslept, and woke with the morning sun streaming into her room. She dressed and hurried downstairs with one decision to tell to Sarah. "Have Rupert pick up an official entry form for the flower show when he goes into London next," Millicent said.

"So you've decided," Sarah said happily.

"Yes, I think it'll be tremendous fun. Of course, now I must decide what to do and start plantings at once," Millicent said. "Something spectacular, a profusion of colors. Any ideas?"

Sarah thought for a moment. "Perhaps a giant,

three-tiered horseshoe of hydrangeas in white, red, and mauve," she offered.

"Go on," Millicent waited.

"A heart in a mixture of colors and textures?"

Millicent shook her head. "Hearts have been done so often," she said. "The newspaper item said that Cynthia Wright had won the last two top awards. See if you can find out what she did."

"That won't be difficult," Sarah said.

"I was thinking perhaps of a giant cornucopia made out of strawflowers, draped over a wire armature, of course," Millicent mused aloud.

"That's interesting," Sarah said. "Strawflowers would be ideal."

"And out of the mouth of the cornucopia, spilling out in a riot of colors, blue gentian, rose campion, peonies, marigolds, pink and yellow buttercups," Millicent said.

"Spectacular indeed," Sarah beamed.

"But I think it's been done before," Millicent frowned.

"You'll do it better," Sarah said.

"I'll keep that in mind while I think a bit more," Millicent said. "First, I must start preparing the garden and the soil. I don't think I've enough good garden soil here to do what I might want to do." She frowned, her eyes narrowed in thought. "I noticed that the Countess has an unused section of garden. I wonder if she'd let me use part of it. I'm going to need a lot of soil and a lot of space in a short time and we can't have growing buds crowding each other."

"Ask her, I'm sure she'd be delighted," Sarah said.

Millicent made that her first project of the day, taking the carriage to the Countess de Berrie that forenoon. "Of course," the Countess said graciously. "The garden is yours. Use as much of it as you need. My soil is really very moist. Underground streams, I believe."

"Good for narcissus and forget-me-nots. Wonderful," Millicent said. "Thank you, so much. I'll make good use of it."

"I'm sure you'll produce a perfectly wonderful entry," the Countess said.

Millicent hurried back to Haddington Hall, her head full of plans, excitement seizing her. She paused to frown at herself. Most young women would have felt excited over their engagement and all the multitude of plans to be made and things to be done before their wedding day. Millicent found the excitement of the flower show really overwhelming the other thoughts in her head. It wasn't a matter of importances at all, she told herself. It was simply that the engagement and all that was to follow would take care of itself, everything falling into place of its own accord, while the entry for the flower show was entirely on her shoulders. The explanation satisfied her and she refused to think about what Sarah would comment on it.

The cornucopia plan was set aside for something

more exciting, which she announced to Sarah one evening after she'd come in from planting rows of hydrangeas. "I shall create a floral picture of Haddington Hall," she said and saw a mixture of dismay and excitement take hold of Sarah's round face.

"That is indeed a project," the woman breathed. "Do you really think you can do it?"

"Yes, I've figured it all out," Millicent said breathlessly as she reconsidered the task. "It will be a floral picture of Haddington Hall, a mosaic of blossoms, flowers instead of needlepoint with an absolute riot of color."

"Marvelous," Sarah murmured, but still she could not help looking dubious. Millicent laughed.

"I'll do it, never fear," she said. The days became as busy as the evenings, what with working in her own garden and making frequent trips to use the Countess's garden plot. Days and evenings melded into one another as Craig continued to be an ardent suitor, almost as though he feared he hadn't really won his prize. Finally, the evening of the Countess de Berrie's gala party arrived.

Millicent arrived with Craig, most of the others already crowding the large ballroom, and the Countess drew her aside at once. "I have been waiting for you," she said. "I'm so delighted at the opportunity to score the social coup of the season. Every hostess wants a party that will be talked about for days. With my announcement, this one will have them talking for months.

She took Millicent's arm, and guided her to one side of the vast room now thronged with colorfully clad gentlemen and ladies, all sparkling as much as their medals, decorations, ribbons, and jewels.

"Dean is here," the Countess whispered to her. "Cynthia Wright brought him as her escort."

Millicent managed not to show either turmoil or anger, though both emotions were instantly whirling through her. She felt her thoughts rushing off with a flurry of speculation. Dean had somehow heard of the announcement the Countess was to make. Perhaps Cynthia Wright had learned of it too and had told him, to her own satisfaction. Total secrets were impossible to keep in the intrigues of London society. He had heard, she repeated again to herself, and he had come to tantalize, mock, flaunt, aware that his very presence would hurt her. She felt the Countess watching her and managed a smile of icy disdain.

"It is of no concern to me whether he's here or not," she said. "I think it rather amusing. Perhaps he's something of a curiosity seeker."

"Good. I feared you might be bothered," the Countess said, her eyes taking on an added twinkle as this new subplot was added to her orchestration. She stepped onto the small, raised section where the string quartet sat, and held up one hand imperiously. Millicent watched all eyes turn toward the tall, commanding figure, and heard the sound of voices diminish to an absolute silence. Millicent's gaze swept the room, and found Cynthia Wright with Dean. She was clinging to his arm a bit desperately, Millicent thought. The girl was pretty in a somewhat colorless manner, pale blue eyes surrounded by very light blond hair. She appeared more washed out beside Dean's intense, dark handsomeness.

"Dear friends and honored guests," she heard the Countess begin. "I have a very special announcement to make on this very special evening. It is no ordinary party when one can tell all of London that one of the most beautiful newcomers to our set and one of the most eligible bachelors have pledged their engagement. I refer to Lady Millicent Hardesty and our own Sir Craig Emlyn."

The room burst into excited shouts, then a ground swell of applause and Millicent saw Craig come through the crowd and step up beside the Countess, bestowing a deep bow and a kiss on her hand. He moved to stand beside Millicent and the crowd surged forward to begin congratulating them both. With the Countess leading her, Millicent stepped from the platform into the throng and it seemed she spent the remainder of the evening accepting excited congratulations from the ladies, warm ones from the gentlemen, and some rueful ones from the young bachelors.

She certainly hadn't planned it, but she suddenly found herself face-to-face with Dean. She frowned, and almost asked him where Cynthia had gone. His eyes burned into her and his jaw muscles throbbed. He looked handsomer than she had ever seen him.

201

The fact sent her anger soaring and all the pain and hurt that still lay inside her flamed at once and she let it become the icy disdain of rage. "You needn't bother with polite words. I abhor pretensions," she said.

"And I abhor stubborn, headstrong stupidity," he bit out, then whirled on his heel and pushed his way through the crowd. She saw him find Cynthia and hurry her from the party. She frowned after him. His words had not been delivered with his usual cool, biting arrogance and she let herself enjoy a moment of satisfaction in that. Perhaps he had suddenly realized that his efforts to secure Haddington Hall were definitely at an end, with no more opportunities for careful deceits left. She heard her name being called, and pushing Dean Fowler from her mind, turned to see Reggie Van Alstine pushing his way toward her.

It was the first time she had seen Reggie since the night at Boodle's and she allowed him a warm smile. "You're looking smashing," he said. "Craig's a deucedly lucky devil, always on the winning side."

Fleetingly, Millicent wondered why young men in this social set made everything sound as though they were talking about a cricket or rugby match. "Luckier than some, I daresay," she remarked. "Peter Humphreys will be able to collect his hundred pounds now," she added, maintaining an air of cool detachment.

"Indeed," Reggie said. "Well, good luck to you both." He kissed her hand and returned to the rest of the party and Millicent found herself surrounded by still other people offering their congratulations. When the evening finally came to a close, she felt herself frowning inwardly. Somehow, she had expected a feeling of greater satisfaction. Perhaps it was only the tiredness pressing upon her, she reasoned as Craig deposited her at her door. He didn't seem a bit tired and held her until she finally insisted he be on his way. She entered the house, pushing open the great door, saw the light in the kitchen, and looked in to find Sarah sipping a cup of tea.

"Couldn't sleep," the older woman said, eyeing the turquoise ball gown with the neckline framed with a *cherusque.* "You look especially elegant tonight," she commented.

"It was an especially elegant evening," Millicent replied. "Our problems are over."

She watched Sarah lift one eyebrow, her eyes waiting. "I've pledged my hand to Craig," Millicent said.

Sarah's lips slowly pursed as her eyes continued to study Millicent. "I see," she said finally and let only silence follow the two words.

"Is that all you're going to say?" Millicent asked, feeling suddenly resentful.

"No, I shall say something more," Sarah replied thoughtfully. "I shall say that I'd be terribly happy for you if you loved Craig Emlyn."

"But of course I love him," Millicent bristled.

"No, you do not," Sarah said with infuriating certainty.

"How can you say that?" Millicent threw back.

"Just look at yourself," Sarah said. "You're all calm, not a bit of excitement about you. You might just as well have told me you were going to Asquith for the races tomorrow. How long have you known about this? Not just this evening, I'll wager."

"Craig asked me a week ago and I agreed," Millicent said. "We decided to say nothing to anyone until the Countess de Berrie's affair this evening. She so wanted to have something spectacular."

"You really wanted to say nothing to me until it was a fait accompli, made public and past changing," Sarah said. "But I'd have known if you'd been in love with Craig Emlyn. You'd have been bubbling about for the past week or been smug as a Cheshire cat. However, you were neither because you're not a young woman in love."

"Don't use that word to me," Millicent said hotly, feeling color flushing her face. "Love is a Judas emotion. It leads you into pain, not happiness. Love is what you make it, and I shall make what I want out of it."

"You can't make anything out of the real thing, my dear," Sarah returned sternly. "It is whatever it is and you can reject it but not deny it. You're trying to deny it. You're fleeing into Craig's arms to spite Dean. This is your way of striking back at him."

"Nonsense," Millicent almost shouted. "And I don't want Dean Fowler's name mentioned in this house again. I told you, he simply doesn't exist for me anymore."

"Yes, so you did," Sarah said, closing her lips tightly. Millicent turned away from her silence that was so voluble, ran up the darkened stairway to her room, and slammed the door behind her. She drew a deep breath, and forced her hands to unclench. Love was one area that Sarah knew little or nothing about, Millicent decided as she quickly undressed. She was full of old-fashioned ideas on the subject, the kind of romantic notions that led only to betrayal and pain.

Millicent slid under the covers. In any case, it was done now, too late for changing. Millicent took the thought to sleep with her as she would a comforting shawl.

CHAPTER NINE

The weekend edition of the London *Times* carried the announcement in the social news columns, emblazoning it with a boldface caption:

LADY MILLICENT HARDESTY AND SIR CRAIG EMLYN BETROTHED

Lady Millicent Hardesty, only recently returned from Australia to reopen Haddington Hall, became the talk of London society today with the announcement of her engagement to Sir Craig Emlyn, one of London's most eligible bachelors. Lady Millicent is a niece of the late Sir Thomas Haddington and Sir Craig is the son of Lord and Lady Emlyn.

A wedding date has not been fixed as yet but all London is beginning to prepare for a round of very smart affairs in connection with the engagement which was announced, informally, by the Countess de Berrie.

Millicent put the newspaper aside with quiet satisfaction, aware that Sarah had already seen it. The subject hadn't been raised again until she had put her arms around Sarah a few days later. "You'll see, I'm doing what's best," Millicent had said.

Sarah's return embrace was instant. "I do hope so, my dear, for your sake," she said. Millicent's calm self-containment stayed unshaken for another day and then, unexpectedly, received two thrusts in as many days. The first was a chance meeting with Reggie Van Alstine as she finished shopping near Guild Hall one afternoon. Just about to step into the clarence, she heard her name called, and saw Reggie passing nearby.

"What brings you to London before dark?" he inquired with a laugh.

"Buying gowns to make me look better after dark," she returned.

"Only the finest shops, though. No catching Lady Millicent in Petticoat Lane, is there?" he said.

"Sometimes. I like a bargain when I can find one," she said, coolly. "I presume Peter Humphreys has collected his hundred pounds by now," she probed.

Reggie let a little frown touch his brow. "Actually,

he hasn't. He tried to collect but he was turned down," Reggie said.

It was Millicent's turn to frown. "Don't tell me Mr. Fowler doesn't pay debts of honor," she said, honestly surprised.

"Peter said he muttered something about not having lost yet," Reggie told her. "Stalked away darkly, then, he did."

Millicent kept her face mildly amused, and allowed a tolerant smile. "No matter," she said. "Good afternoon," going on into the carriage hastily and pulling the door shut after her. She sank back in the seat, a frown digging into her brow. Dean had always been given to cryptic statements, she told herself. Perhaps he was simply unable to admit to himself that he'd lost his clever little campaign. She let herself cling to the explanation, even as she felt an unreasoning stab of fear.

The second incident involved Craig as they walked through Kensington Park in the afternoon, the sun through the leaves making little dappled patterns of light. "I've convinced mother to have a positively smashing bash for the first of the month," he said. "Practically all of Parliament will be there. We can announce a wedding date then."

"Convinced?" Millicent echoed, picking up the word at once. Perhaps too quickly, she realized as Craig looked uncomfortable for an instant. Uncharacteristically, she wasn't bothered by his discomfort.

"Mother wasn't in favor, I'll admit," he said. "She wanted us to wait till December before announcing a wedding date."

"December? What in heavens for?" Millicent asked with studied innocence as she remembered the subtle inquisition Lady Emlyn had conducted at their first meeting. The woman hadn't been satisfied that afternoon and it was apparent she was still less than happy. "We had discussed next month, darling," Millicent said, pressing his hand. "Remember?"

"Yes, I know. Mother's just a bit put out because I'm finally getting married. You know how some mothers are about such things. She doesn't really favor it, but I'll handle her," he said.

The little knot forming in the pit of Millicent's stomach was not dissolved by Craig's airy confidence. She remembered Lady Emlyn's steely cold politeness all too well. Millicent let her leg move to rest against Craig's knee. "I don't want to wait one day more than next month, darling," she said.

She saw a glow form in Craig's eyes, unalloyed anticipation. "Next month it will be, I promise you," he said.

Millicent gave him a smile that would melt the resolve of a saint, and the remainder of the evening passed without further mention of Lady Emlyn's reluctant cooperation. Later, alone in her room, Millicent found she could dismiss the woman's hanging back with much greater ease than she could Dean

Fowler's cryptic remark on the wager. It continued to stick in her mind and made her quietly furious for being unable to shake it loose. But then his remarks had a way of doing just that, she reminded herself. Time would dismiss it, she decided. Time and the growing nearness of the flower show. Her blooms were coming up marvelously well, both those in her own garden and those at the Countess's. It was with renewed excitement and added determination that she worked on her entry. Sarah had learned about Cynthia Wright's winning entry of the year before.

"Starburst of roses, multicolored blooms," Sarah reported. "Very big and very eye-catching, I was told. And her blooms were excellent specimens."

"We'll do better," Millicent promised. Her project entailed a certain logistical aspect that she had to plan with absolute accuracy. It was impossible to move a huge floral picture in one piece so she had a collection of open-faced, flat boxes made and filled with soil. Carefully cut, they were designed to fit together and were movable and she directed the construction of each one as carefully as she grew her blossoms.

She was in the garden one morning when the daily post was brought to her. She opened a letter from the Upsham sisters. It was an invitation to a tea and she made a face. Time was growing short, the date of the flower show beginning to press upon her. But it would never do to decline the invitation and she accepted with something less than enthusiasm. The

Countess was there when she arrived and answered her question about the reason for the tea.

"Gloria and Glovina have found an obscure poet they want to make less obscure. They enjoy playing patronesses," she said, sweeping away with a regality befitting a queen. Millicent turned, aware of eyes on her, and found Cynthia Wright watching her. Automatically, Millicent felt herself glance around the room to see if Dean were there. He wasn't, of course, there being no gentlemen at all at the tea and the instant reaction made her fume at herself. Cynthia Wright moved toward her, the girl's pale eyes revealing nothing.

"You've entered the flower show," the girl commented.

"You do keep informed," Millicent said.

"Yes," Cynthia agreed. "I also hear you're preparing something unusual."

"We'll see when the time comes, won't we?" Millicent smiled. "You won't have terribly long to wait."

"Neither will you, my dear," the girl said and drifted off. Millicent turned away, bothered by the girl's attitude. There was something distastefully smug in it. But the meeting did have some positive aspects. It sent her back to her gardens and preparations with renewed determination to see that Cynthia Wright did not win a third Grand Prize. The week that followed passed all too quickly between her flowers and Craig. She had almost stopped thinking about Dean Fowler in relation to Haddington Hall.

212

Indeed, she'd quite dismissed his presence as a threat. It was over and he had lost his attempt to usurp her rights.

Therefore, the letter, when it arrived, came with the shock of the totally unexpected. Millicent was in the study opening the morning post and expected it to be just another congratulatory note. So many continued to arrive that it was obvious many people were late in receiving their social news. She opened the envelope, stared at the stationery, amd her eyes grew round as saucers. "Sarah!" she screamed as she sank onto the edge of the nearest chair.

Sarah appeared at once. Millicent's eyes were still rooted to the letter she held in one trembling hand. "Good Lord, what is it, my dear?" Sarah questioned.

"This," Millicent gasped out. "This letter from Mr. Ackrood. I don't believe it. I just don't believe it." She thrust the letter at Sarah, her eyes wide with shock. "Read it for yourself."

Sarah took the letter, and peered at it closely. The careful phrases lifted from the paper, accusing yet not indicting, commenting without comment:

My Dear Lady Hardesty,

I am in receipt of a disturbing letter from Mr. Dean Fowler, whom you know is now your neighbor and was a friend of your late uncle, Sir Thomas.

Mr. Fowler has sent me a copy of the letter from Sir Thomas to him. While this letter has moral considerations implicit in it, it is also of some legal consequence. More disturbing in relation to the letter is Mr. Fowler's statement that you have no legitimate claim to Haddington Hall. He professes to be able to prove this.

Can you kindly send me substantive material to answer these charges?

Respectfully,
Robert Ackrood, Esquire

Sarah's lips pursed as she studied the letter for another moment. Then, glancing at Millicent, she saw the young woman's ashen face. "A very determined man, your Dean Fowler," Sarah observed.

"He's not *my* Dean Fowler," Millicent shot back, anger intruding on her shock. She took the letter as Sarah handed it back, and stared at it. It certainly explained his cryptic remarks to Peter Humphreys and his refusal to pay the wager. Did his arrogance know no bounds, she fumed silently. But anger gave way to a whirl of apprehension and her eyes found Sarah's once again.

"What can I do? Do you think he has any proof?" she asked. "How could he? He doesn't know that much about me. I think he's just trying to bully me," Millicent added without waiting for Sarah's answer. "I shall dismiss him and his accusations out of hand."

"That's one way to answer. It's worth a try," Sarah agreed.

"Call Rupert. I shall have him deliver my reply to Mr. Ackrood in person. It will be written and sealed by the time Rupert brings the carriage," Millicent said. She sat down at the writing desk as Sarah left, and wrote a trio of lines on the notepaper, her sharp, strong letters reflecting the anger she felt.

Dear Mr. Ackrood,

You may ignore the letter from Mr. Dean Fowler. He is consumed with personal malice and has resorted to wild accusations. Pay him no heed.

Respectfully,
Lady Millicent Hardesty

She handed the letter to the driver when he appeared, and drew a deep breath as she watched him hurry out to the carriage. "So much for Mr. Dean Fowler," she said to Sarah. "That's the man you wanted me to listen to again? He's ruthless, mean, and spiteful as well as deceitful. I hate him."

"I must say he is affording me some unpleasant surprises," Sarah said. "And I always prided myself on being able to read character. Well, let's wait and see if your answer to Mr. Ackrood is sufficient."

Millicent nodded in agreement and tried to put aside the apprehension that had seized her. "Nobody will believe him," she said and wished she felt as convinced as she sounded. "I've passed all the hurdles, been accepted by those who count in the social set," Millicent thought aloud. Perhaps it had been done with mirrors, but it was done, she told herself. And the engagement to Craig loomed even larger, now, lending her a greater status. No, there was nothing to fear. Dean was simply trying to strike at her. That gave its own satisfaction. Perhaps more than his imperiousness had been touched. Perhaps he had been hurt. Good, she sniffed silently. He deserved it.

"Better get dressed," she heard Sarah say. "Isn't Craig calling for you in an hour?"

"Yes, I'd forgotten," Millicent gasped and flew up the stairs. He had arranged an afternoon call on his mother to discuss the smashing reception he had "convinced" her to give. The truth, as Millicent determined by his slightly uncomfortable insistence, was that he had not really convinced Lady Emlyn of anything. Without saying so in direct words, he was hoping Millicent's presence might help and so she had graciously agreed to go. The results were as important to her as to Craig. Especially now, she murmured meaningfully.

She'd just finished dressing when Craig arrived.

She met him in a redingote of gray silk, buttoned all the way down the front with a very high, white collar. It was the only truly conservative gown she owned and she didn't much care for it but decided it might be in order for the meeting. She wore an aigrette in her hair to soften the severity of her costume. Lady Emlyn was waiting for her in the drawing room, an ornate, silver tea service laid out on a dark-blue cloth.

Craig hovered nervously nearby, not unlike an uncertain gladiator, she decided, but she felt some sympathy for his position. Defying or even contradicting his mother was a seldom taken role for him.

Lady Emlyn wasted no time on small talk.

"As Craig has no doubt told you," she began, "his Lordship and I prefer you both to wait until December to announce a wedding date. Craig has insisted on next month. I can only presume that his strong feelings are a reflection of yours," the woman said.

Millicent refused to rise to the challenge in the remark. "I'm afraid they are," she said demurely, letting her hand touch Craig's arm with a note of possessiveness. "Though I would be just as happy with a simple announcement rather than a large party."

"How considerate of you," the woman said, turning the compliment into a barb. "Tell me, my dear, did you attend the great affairs the Aldersons gave in Australia?"

The question, coming with total unexpectedness,

took Millicent by surprise. She took a moment to recover, her mind racing to find an answer. "I was never friendly with the Aldersons," she said.

"I see. I thought perhaps you really favored the large gathering," the woman said. "You were never friendly with the Aldersons yet your companion, Sarah Elkins, worked for them, is that right?"

"Why, yes, that is so," Millicent said. "I hired her after she had left the Aldersons."

"Rather unusual for a woman to leave good employment in a country where there are such few opportunities for similar positions, isn't it?" Lady Emlyn asked.

Millicent half-shrugged. "That really was none of my concern," she answered.

"You didn't know the Apthorns or the Davenports then, did you?" the woman asked, fastening her with a cold eye.

Millicent felt her uneasiness growing. The woman's questions were more pointed than last time. She forced a smile. "I'm wondering if that is a question or a statement," she sparred.

"A little of both, I daresay. I received a letter from Harriet Davenport yesterday," Lady Emlyn said. Millicent held her smile as she wondered if it had been a letter in answer to inquiries or simply a bit of correspondence.

"No, I'm afraid I know neither the Davenports nor the Apthorns," Millicent said.

"Strange, seeing as how they're both so prominent

in Australian society, a pitifully small group indeed," the woman said.

"Perhaps they've not been active in recent years," Millicent offered.

"Perhaps," Lady Emlyn said but her tone indicated that she disagreed entirely. Millicent felt tiny quiverings inside her stomach. The woman had definitely become more probing. Was it simply resentment at losing Craig, she wondered. Or was it something else? Millicent admonished herself silently. She was seeing shadows, and she refused to permit that. She met Lady Emlyn's eyes boldly, and let a smile cover the directness of her words.

"I should terribly much enjoy discussing my social life in Australia with you, Lady Emlyn, but at another time. I understood we were here to discuss the plans for an announcement of the wedding date," she said, casting a quick glance at Craig. He looked faintly uncomfortable.

"Yes, of course. I suppose we must get to that, mustn't we," the woman said, making it sound like a disagreeable chore one must set about to do. "Craig insists on a large, fancy party for the announcement, but of course you are aware of that," the woman said. Lady Emlyn was really an expert in genteel skewering, Millicent decided and held down the anger that began to stir inside her. It was time for cleverness and caution, not anger, but she couldn't help wondering if news of Dean Fowler's accusations had somehow reached the woman.

"I repeat, I am perfectly willing to go along with whatever Craig and you think is best," Millicent said.

"I'm standing for a really big bash," Craig said and Millicent felt irritatedly grateful that he had finally deigned to make a definitive statement. At that, he couldn't help but look dubious, she noted, anxiously glancing at his mother. "After all, one doesn't get married every day, does one?" Craig laughed, unable to disguise the effort in his attempt at levity.

Lady Emlyn refused him even a smile. "I suppose we will have to go along with Craig's wishes," she said, and Millicent caught the omission of her desires as any factor in the decision. She maintained her smile and knew that Lady Emlyn was not a friend. She wondered if the woman would ever like her and decided she didn't care terribly one way or the other. Lord Emlyn arrived at the house just as Millicent and Craig were leaving and he greeted her with a perfunctory enthusiasm. Yet, on balance, the quiet ordeal had ended successfully, with Craig's wishes being acceded to in the end.

"I should like to beg off dinner, darling," Millicent told him. "I'm really awfully tired." It was no lie and he accepted the change of plans with only modest disappointment. Once at home, Millicent went to her room, more exhausted than she should have been. She slept poorly, and finally rose to the new day feeling tense and irritable. Thoughts of Dean and his arrogant persistence had drifted in and out of her dreams all night and that angered her. She expected more loyalty of her dreams, certainly less insubordination.

When she went downstairs, a letter from Mr. Ackrood was waiting for her, as was Sarah. She went into the study with Sarah and closed the door. There was nothing to be gained by the servants overhearing. Her eyes scanned the script and once again a mixture of fear and fury fought inside her. The letter was less carefully phrased this time.

My Dear Lady Hardesty,

I am afraid I cannot simply pay Mr. Fowler no heed, as you somewhat peremptorily suggested. He has raised serious legal questions which involve not only Haddington Hall but my proper duties as legal counsel for the late Sir Thomas.

I must ask you to meet with me for a full review of this entire matter and to bring with you, at that time, a fully documented set of proofs of your claims to Haddington Hall and your genealogical relationship to Sir Thomas.

Respectfully,
Robert Ackrood, Esquire

P.S. I shall be at Mr. Fowler's home the afternoon of the tenth. If it is more convenient for you than a trip to London, you may meet me there.

Millicent's eyes were clouded with apprehension as she stared at Sarah. "What shall I do? What can I do?" she asked.

"What do you want to do, Millicent?" Sarah asked in return.

"Fight. Prove him wrong," Millicent said at once, but just as quickly, her face falling in dismay, she added, "Except that I don't know that I can. I did stretch the truth, as you know, and I don't have a family pedigree that will prove anything. I mean, it is all rather on the thin side, as you well know."

Sarah's lips pursed as she thought, making no reply for a few moments. Finally, she gathered her words. "I think you'll have to try to brazen it through, just as we've done up until now. We've done rather well, so far, as you know."

"And if I can't brazen it out?" Millicent queried dismally.

"We shall cross that bridge when we come to it," Sarah said. "First thing is for you to meet with Mr. Ackrood, and, I presume, Dean Fowler. Go and listen to what Dean has to say. You know, he may be just trying to whistle up a storm without any real evidence, himself. Find out first hand, stand up to him, and then we'll decide what we can do."

"All right," Millicent said. "We shall do exactly

that." She glanced at the letter again. "The afternoon of the tenth. That's the day after the flower show. Good. I shall not let that interfere with the show." She flashed an angry glance at Sarah. "I'll meet the good Mr. Ackrood at Dean's house. If I'm to be upset, I'd rather it be close to home than in London."

"Why not send word to Dean Fowler to come here with Mr. Ackrood?" Sarah suggested. "You might feel more secure here if you must do battle."

Millicent flared up at once. "Absolutely not. I won't have Dean Fowler set foot in Haddington Hall. I can just see him now, looking about with that possessive attitude of his, taking in this and that with covetous eyes. No, never, not here. I shall keep him as far away from Haddington Hall as I can." Millicent folded the letter and put it in a desk drawer. "Now let me bring my attention back to preparing for the show. That will take all of my energies now," she said.

The first step of the final preparation was to transplant the flowers she had chosen from the garden into the special open-topped, soil-filled boxes, following the lines of the blueprint she had made for each box. Millicent had decided to make her huge, floral needlepoint picture of Haddington Hall out of Michaelmas daisies for the outer borders, their lavender beauty both delicate and strong. Deep red carnations and white hydrangea were used to form the lower portions of the picture, their strength of color giving strength of line. Cornflowers were used for the windows with peony window boxes. Grass and ground were lily of the valley, rooflines of evening primrose. The entire floral picture was enclosed in a giant frame of thousands of French marigold buds.

The night before the show Thornbury Hall was given over to the entrants bringing in and setting up their displays. Millicent had hired four large fruit rack wagons to carry the soil boxes with their transplanted lines of flowers. Sarah by her side, she went in the clarence, leading the line of wagons. Once inside Thornbury Hall there began the last and most important task, laying down the soil boxes, fitting them together properly, following the numbers Millicent had given each one.

But it was done finally, only a little before midnight, and Sarah stepped back to take in the full magnificence of the work. "Absolutely marvelous, my dear," she breathed. "A spectacular concept, beautifully executed, a natural palette of color."

Sarah took her arm, and they returned to the carriage for the ride back to Haddington Hall. "You need sleep. Tomorrow will be an exciting day, regardless of how it turns out," she said. The words were prophetic as, in the morning, Millicent returned to Thornbury Hall to view the other entries that had arrived during the night. She found Cynthia Wright's quickly, the girl standing in front of it, and let her eyes take in the huge floral vase fashioned mostly of mauve hydrangea and decorated with the brilliant red of trumpet honeysuckle, a base bordered by the rich gold of winter daffodil. It was perhaps nine feet high, terribly impressive, yet compared with her creation, it paled, Millicent decided.

The judges arrived during the afternoon, all staid, unsmiling members of the Board of Governors of the Royal Horticultural Society. The crowd of visitors followed them about as they went from entry to entry and watched them make little notes in identical writing tablets each carried. They were slow and thorough, but by late afternoon they had finished. Millicent tried desperately to stay calm, but felt the tension gripping her as the time to announce the winner arrived. One of the judges, a man with a short, black Vandyke, mounted a small podium to make the announcement.

"Entry number twenty, the entry of Lady Millicent Hardesty," he said. "Grand Prize winner for this year."

Millicent could not stop the smile of pure glee that flooded her face as applause broke out. She stepped forward toward the judge, now flanked by the other judges. She had just reached him when a voice cut through the murmur of the onlookers.

"Protest, please," the voice called out. "Protest."

Millicent turned, frowning, and saw Cynthia Wright making her way forward. Dean was just behind her, his intense face tight, his jaw held stiffly. Cynthia halted before the judges. "Rule number eleven of the contest requirements state that each entry must be a product of the entrant's personal

225

garden," she read from a small copy of the rules she held in one hand.

"It does," the judge said. "That is to eliminate professional floral decorators or entrants combining their talents."

"The Lady Hardesty's entry was not raised solely in her own gardens," the girl said smugly.

The judges turned their collective gaze at Millicent and she swallowed, then found her voice. "Some of my blooms were raised in the Countess de Berrie's garden," she admitted.

"I see," the man with the Vandyke murmured.

"I didn't have enough space of my own," Millicent tried to explain. "I did it all myself. The Countess was not involved."

"The rules are most clear," Cynthia put in. "My protest remains."

"You are talking about a minor technicality here," Millicent objected.

"That's a matter of opinion. Without the use of the Countess's garden you may not have been able to mount such a large entry," the girl said coldly. "Technicality or not, the rules are quite explicit and your entry is in violation of them."

"Please excuse the committee for a few minutes," the judge said and Millicent saw him gather the others in a corner. Their discussion was quiet but intense and finally they returned. The spokesman mounted the little podium again.

"Unfortunately, the judges feel they are bound by

the rules of the contest and the rules state their intent without exception. The entry cannot come from other than the entrant's personal garden. Protest is allowed and the award withdrawn," he said.

Millicent pressed her lips together and nodded at the man. She would not make a public debate of it. They had done their duty as they saw it and were not to be blamed. She was the victim of a technicality. And a maliciously smug rival. She turned to Cynthia Wright as the crowd buzzed with talk, and met the girl's taunting eyes.

"You can't play fast and loose with rules, my dear," the girl said.

"The Lady Millicent is adept at just that," she heard Dean say, and met his dark, angry eyes.

"Would you care to explain that insulting remark?" she flung at him.

"In time," he muttered. "In time." He turned on his heels and strode away. He was obviously as unconcerned with Cynthia Wright's feelings as her own, she noted, and was surprised at the unwarranted satisfaction that thought seemed to give her. She was still frowning when she left Thornbury Hall and climbed into the clarence for the trip back to Haddington Hall. The Countess and a few others had come to her before she left to voice their condolences at the outcome. Millicent could only shrug. "I shall have to read rules more carefully in the future," she said. Of course, she hadn't read these at all.

She returned to the great house and told Sarah

what had happened, not hiding her disappointment at the decision and her fury at Dean's remark. "What do you think he has up his sleeve?" she asked, suddenly worried.

"We'll see soon enough," Sarah answered.

"Whatever it is, he won't get away with it," Millicent flared, suddenly terribly tired. "I'm going up and rest some," she told Sarah and the older woman nodded in understanding. Millicent undressed in her room, grateful that there was absolutely nothing social on the calendar before the time to meet with Mr. Ackrood and Dean. She was equally grateful that Craig had been called away on a trip to Birmingham and hadn't been home for the show. She didn't think she could have stood his eager sympathies. Defeat, even an undeserved one, is often better met with alone. Or in the company of those who had that special ability to comfort without obsequiousness and there were few of those about.

More importantly, she would use the time to prepare for the meeting. She rested during the afternoon and in the evening set to the task of trying to remember all the family facts she could remember, especially about Uncle Thomas. Ackrood wanted some kind of proof and she hoped enough details about family life might satisfy his cautious, legal mind.

But she found, unhappily, that there were precious few facts she could muster. Recountings of holiday dinners would hardly fit the barrister's definition of facts. Guests at those occasions could have the same stories to recount. She had, up to now, fashioned a role and a history for herself, all of it a charade and charades do not rewrite facts, only the semblance of them. Hers had been a monumental charade, pieces constructed out of whole cloth with only the barest skeleton of fact beneath the surface.

She went to bed tired, suddenly aware that searching one's memory can be exhausting, and more so when one is searching through a wasteland of fact. She felt her lips press grimly together as she lay in the big bed. She had come this far most successfully, so much so that the charade had been transformed into reality. Dean Fowler was trying a last bit of desperate underhandedness, she told herself. He'd nothing more than that. She turned on her side and wished she was better able to convince herself. She was tired, she reflected, and fatigue made for self-doubts. She forced herself to sleep but when morning came, uneasiness was still upon her. She dressed hurriedly, and sought out Sarah downstairs.

"You must come with me," Millicent said.

"Might it not look a bit odd?" Sarah asked. "I am your companion, and I've been at the balls at your side when you've given them here. But this is a business meeting."

"I don't much care how it looks to Dean Fowler or Robert Ackrood, my reluctant barrister, and there'll not be anyone else there," Millicent insisted. "I need you with me. I feel I'm going in naked. Besides, I want you to hear whatever is said for yourself. We may have to put our heads together afterward."

"I'll get my things," Sarah agreed.

"I'll feel foolish taking the clarence but I'm not walking over there, either," Millicent muttered, gathering her own things. Rupert made the slow circle from her driveway, which led to Dean's property, as though it were a lengthy journey. A butler ushered her and Sarah into the library. Dean, standing very straight and tall, wore a light green embroidered riding jacket with a ruffled shirt and met her quick glance. His face was set, tight, yet without the imperiousness she had expected. His intense, handsome countenance reached out to her and she felt the twisting inside herself. She looked away from him to nod at Robert Ackrood. The spidery, tall figure, clothed in a formal afternoon coat with a pearl-gray foulard, his concession to informality, no doubt, half-bowed.

Sarah unobtrusively positioned herself near the straight-backed chair obviously left for Millicent, whose eyes swept the room again, cool hauteur in every movement. She halted, resting her glance on Dean, and felt her hands tremble. She hated him and his terrible handsomeness, hated how just standing before her he could make her quiver inside.

"If you and I could have a few private moments to talk, perhaps this meeting could be amicably settled," Dean said, his eyes burning into hers.

"I hardly think so," Millicent answered. "If you

really have anything to say, you may do so right here in front of Mr. Ackrood. Indeed, your suggestion leads me to believe that you have nothing to back your wild accusations."

"You're very wrong but I'd prefer to talk to you than have to back them," he tried again.

"But I, sir, have no desire whatever to listen to you in private," Millicent returned icily, beginning to believe that he had actually been bluffing. She'd just call his bluff, then.

Dean, his lips turning into a thin, angry line, his face darkening, turned to the barrister. "Lady Millicent had no proper claim to Haddington Hall," he bit out.

"Preposterous. Words, all empty words," Millicent flung at him, taking in Mr. Ackrood in a sweeping glance.

"She hasn't even any right to use the appellation *Lady* Millicent," Dean speared.

"How dare you?" Millicent shot back, letting her apparent anger cover the fright that exploded inside her. She turned to the barrister. "I can give you a dozen of the leading members of London society who know of my right to that title."

"A dozen easily excited individuals who are just as easily taken in and who *know* nothing at all," Dean returned.

"Mr. Fowler, do you have some evidence of these accusations?" Robert Ackrood interrupted.

"Indeed. I went to the College of Arms and had

them go through the entire genealogical records of the Haddington family. They had embarked upon that as a matter of course after *Lady* Millicent had asked permission to use the Haddington crest. I gave their search added momentum. You are aware of the rules governing family relationships in regard to the use of a family crest and the claim of family privileges, are you not, Mr. Ackrood?"

"Yes, of course. Only direct descendants in listed genealogical lines are eligible and their descendants by marriage, provided the marriage contains at least one member of pure, close lineage," the barrister said.

"Very distant nieces, fringe family members, do not come under those eligibility rules," Dean said.

"True, but I originally wrote to Madam Hardesty because there was a mention in the family records of her husband and herself, she being noted in the mention of the marriage as a Haddington," Mr. Ackrood explained.

"Yes, so there is. But according to the College of Arms the relationship is entirely too distant to qualify as direct family, which leaves Millicent Hardesty with no right to use the Haddington crest and no right to the appellation of Lady Haddington, to say nothing of Lady Hardesty, which seems to be a pure invention," Dean flung out with undisguised triumph.

Millicent felt herself shriveling inside, his words cruel, biting, slashing at her as she listened. He had amassed facts, rules and regulations, restrictions and traditions which she could not answer. A wave of helplessness swept over her. If there was a counter-claim to Dean's words, she hadn't the facts at her fingertips to fling back at him. Worse yet, there were most likely no facts to fling back. Her eyes found Sarah's and she saw the older woman's glance boring into her, trying to send courage, a message to fight back. A delaying action, Millicent murmured silently. That was all she could do now. She drew in a deep breath, and turned to face Mr. Ackrood.

"I did not expect to be insulted in this manner," she said. "I shall not give Mr. Fowler the satisfaction of defending myself against his preposterous accusations. That would be playing into his hands, giving him more stories to tell to his friends in the smoke-filled rooms of Boodle's." She rose, glared at Dean for an instant, then returned her glance to Mr. Ackrood, who looked unsatisfied and unhappy, his long face stretching downward not unlike a dyspeptic bloodhound.

"But Lady Hardesty, I do need some evidence, some facts to rebut Mr. Fowler's claims," he complained with almost a whining note in his voice.

"And you shall have them," Millicent snapped. "But not here, not to furnish Mr. Fowler with more enjoyment of this shoddy moment." She sounded terribly righteous, almost enough to convince herself, and a sudden thought flashed into her mind. She fastened the barrister with a cold stare. "Do you think I would have restored Haddington Hall to all its gracious beauty if I were some kind of imposter? That, my dear sir, cannot be done by anyone. It requires caring, an appreciation, a kind of love."

She saw the lawyer glance questioningly at Dean, and let her eyes flick to the strong, handsome face. He surprised her again, taking her off-balance once more. "Yes, I believe it did require that," Dean said slowly. "The care taken to bring Haddington Hall back to all its beauty was probably the only honest act in Lady Millicent's clever campaign."

Millicent felt the pain in her stomach, as though she'd been physically struck. "I hate you," she hissed, immediately sorry she'd allowed her feelings to show. She turned to Mr. Ackrood, putting on her grandest and most regal glance. "I shall be in further touch with you on this matter, Mr. Ackrood," she said. "You may be assured of that." She spun on her heel, motioned for Sarah to follow, and swept from the room. "Good day, Mr. Ackrood," she called over her shoulder.

"Magnificent," she heard Dean's voice boom out after her. "A truly magnificent performance."

Millicent's eyes were stinging as she hurled herself into the carriage and pressed back against the seat as Sarah followed her in. Anguish in her eyes, Millicent nonetheless motioned for silence until Rupert had guided the carriage the short trip to Haddington Hall once again. It was only when she and Sarah were behind the closed doors of the study that she let words of fury and despair tumble from her. "He's despicable, quite worse than I'd ever imagined him to be," she said.

"He's also been very thorough in his research," Sarah said. "He's certainly determined to get Haddington Hall." The older woman reflected a moment. "A strange combination of characteristics, that intense man," she murmured.

"All hateful," Millicent snapped.

"He seemed to thoroughly understand your love for Haddington Hall, though," Sarah remarked.

"He was just trying another tack for a moment," Millicent retorted. Her face became a mask of dismay. "Isn't there anything I can do? Perhaps contact the College of Arms?"

"Never. They make their august decisions after studying submitted documents. Strangely enough, I do believe you might well have a legitimate claim. There are no Haddingtons left of direct descendancy, and though Dean was completely right about the College of Arms's position on these matters, you could petition them for a hearing under special circumstances."

"Then I shall do that," Millicent said.

Sarah looked grim. "I fear the facts make that move academic. Time is on Dean Fowler's side. It would take the College up to two years to study your petition. They'll take that long to completely research the entire matter, then perhaps another six months to reach a decision. Two-and-a-half years, my dear. Your exchequer will let you maintain Haddington Hall for another two-and-a-half months, I estimate. You've neither the time nor the funds to fight it out."

"And Dean Fowler suspects as much," Millicent bit out.

"I'm afraid so. Then there's the good barrister Ackrood. He doesn't want his original actions made the object of questioning by his peers. He will press for a resolution and certainly leap at every chance for one," Sarah said.

"Then what can I do?" Millicent asked in despair.

"I don't know, except that you must give Mr. Ackrood some kind of answer."

"I shall write him in high indignation," Millicent said. "Perhaps I can bully him into backing down. Or at least turning away from Dean Fowler's pressure."

"I don't know that it will satisfy him but I suppose it's all you have," Sarah conceded. She left, frowning into space, and Millicent drank a glass of sherry to calm herself before sitting down to compose a letter to Mr. Ackrood. She made a first draft, found it too verbose, put it aside, and went to bed. In the morning, she rewrote it, then made a third, final letter. It sounded terribly hollow, she admitted as she read it over to herself, yet she had only bombast as a weapon.

Dear Mr. Ackrood,

I must demand that you disregard the unfounded, spiteful, and ungentlemanly accusations of Mr. Dean Fowler. You know the genealogical facts of my relationship to Sir Thomas. That should be sufficient.

Thank you,
Lady Hardesty

She sealed it with a displeased shrug and posted it in London that evening when she attended the Featherstone gala with Craig. She tried unsuccessfully to put the matter out of her thoughts but kept seeing Dean's tight-lipped face as he flung accusations at her. She blamed the matter for her general unhappiness with Craig throughout the evening. He had too much champagne, she thought, and his wit seemed particularly superficial. It was her dark inner mood, of course, she murmured to herself.

The answer from Mr. Ackrood arrived only two days later in the form of the barrister's spindly presence. "I thought a personal visit was in order," he explained, his face as dour as a Scottish moor in a rainstorm. Millicent ushered him into the study and asked Sarah to join them. "I fear I can't simply disregard Mr. Fowler's accusations as you ask," the barrister said.

"Why not?" Millicent thrust haughtily.

"First, he has filed a formal action against your claims with the College. He has presented me with the substance of this action. As the position of the College of Arms in these instances is a matter of public record, it is almost certain that they will disallow your claim to direct family descendancy," Mr. Ackrood said. He drew a deep sigh before going on. "Legally, then, I am bound to act upon the stated wishes of Sir Thomas in the absence of a direct family heir."

"Which is?" Millicent interrupted.

"The substance of the letter he wrote to Mr. Fowler," the attorney said. "In truth, my hands are tied in this matter. I am bound to correct any error I may have made in the original handling of this affair."

"It seems to me you are more fearful of being judged in error than in helping me or Sir Thomas," Millicent snapped. Mr. Ackrood looked increasingly uncomfortable and started to murmur protests, which Millicent rode over peremptorily. "I want you to tell me how I may protect my interests in Haddington Hall," she thrust at him.

He shrugged unhappily. "I'm afraid only by supplying me with a detailed, documented brief satisfactorily countering Mr. Fowler's statements," he answered.

"And if that is an impossible task, or if I choose not to do so?" Millicent pressed.

"Then I must disallow your claims to Haddington Hall and allow Mr. Fowler to purchase it at the fair market value," the barrister said. "That is the law."

"You are really telling me there is nothing at all

I can do, in view of the long-held position of the College of Arms in regard to such claims," Millicent summed up angrily. "I could enter a formal counter-claim to the College. That would send everything into a state of temporary suspension."

"Yes, and it would take years," the lawyer said, grimacing, echoing Sarah's words. He then added another note of despair. "In that event, I could not let you or Mr. Fowler occupy the premises, but as you are the claimant of ownership, you would be liable for all taxes and maintenance expenses." Millicent exchanged a quick glance of anguish with Sarah as Mr. Ackrood frowned into space. "There is one more thing," he murmured. "You could submit a purchase price for Haddington Hall yourself."

"I could what?" Millicent frowned.

"Purchase Haddington Hall," the barrister repeated. "If you outbid Mr. Fowler, it would all be reduced to a simple matter of my having to accept the highest bidder."

Millicent stared at the long-faced man for another moment. "Yes, I see," she murmured slowly. "And it would neatly take you off the hook, as it were, wouldn't it?" she speared. The man half-shrugged. "Good day, Mr. Ackrood," Millicent said curtly, "I shall be in touch."

When the barrister left, she whirled to face Sarah's rueful face. "A way out that is beyond your taking," Sarah said. "An answer that is really no answer at all." But Millicent's eyes were suddenly sparkling.

"On the contrary. It is the very answer I need," she said. Sarah's round face formed a frown. "The irony of it swept over me as he was talking," Millicent said. "I couldn't help thinking back to that first letter the good barrister sent that day in Toowoomba. It was a gift that seemed no gift at all, remember? And here he was doing much the same thing, offering answers that seem no answers at all."

"Yes, but then you had the shop to sell. The proceeds of that made everything else possible. You had a trump card, then," Sarah answered.

"And I have one, now," Millicent announced. "I shall simply purchase Haddington Hall. Dean Fowler is a man of modest wealth. I will outbid him." She saw Sarah's glance take on concern and wary apprehension. "No, I haven't gone mad," Millicent said. "I shall have Craig purchase it for me. He's been begging me to tell him what I want as a wedding present. Something grand, he keeps saying. Now the whole matter is as good as finished."

Millicent watched Sarah nod, her face drawing into itself, the roundness managing to become square. "Is there something wrong in that?" Millicent demanded.

Sarah paused, then answered, her voice flat. "Selling a shop and trading off yourself are two very different things," she answered.

"What a perfectly horrid thing to say," Millicent gasped.

"Is it?" Sarah asked. "I still say you don't love

Craig Emlyn. I saw your eyes when you faced Dean the other day, a moment only, but long enough."

"You imagined whatever you thought you saw," Millicent said hotly. "Why can't you believe that I love Craig?" she asked in angry exasperation.

"An old woman's intuition," Sarah said gently.

"Well, your old woman's intuition is quite wrong," Millicent snapped.

Sarah's smile was quietly wry. "Perhaps," she allowed.

"I shall take care of everything tonight," Millicent said with undisguised triumph. "Haddington Hall and Mr. Dean Fowler's underhanded arrogance."

"A last bold venture, is it?" Sarah remarked.

"You may call it that if you wish," Millicent answered loftily. "Except this one will be much easier to accomplish."

Sarah made no comment and Millicent decided she was just being stubborn, and unwilling to admit as much. Sweeping from the room, Millicent went upstairs and indulged in a long, warm bath to relax, then finally began to dress. She was waiting when Craig arrived. She didn't bring the matter up till the evening was near an end and Craig's advances were growing more amorous. And annoying. The thought bothered Millicent. One really oughtn't to be annoyed by the advances of the man to whom one was engaged. It was all this business with Haddington Hall, she told herself. It had put her on edge.

"I've found that grand wedding gift you can give

241

me, darling," she said, removing Craig's hand as it stole dangerously near her bodice.

"Wonderful," he said brightly. "Let's have it."

"Haddington Hall," she said, and watched his frown gather at once.

"But you already own Haddington Hall," he said.

"Yes, but there's been a bit of legal chicanery. Your friend, Dean Fowler, has mounted a set of perfectly preposterous claims against my right to Haddington Hall. He has a letter from Sir Thomas that he's also using to bolster his arguments."

"My heavens," Craig muttered, and frowned into space. "That is an unexpected turn of events, isn't it."

"Of course, he's mounted a set of lies and half-truths but I haven't time to enter into all this terrible legal folderol. The important thing is that it can all be put to an end by your simply purchasing Haddington Hall for me at whatever is the right bid. Of course, it will be ours, anyway, in time."

Craig's eyes met hers. "Yes, if that would end the matter, I certainly would want to do it for you, my love, but the hard truth is that I don't really have that kind of money."

It was Millicent's turn to frown in surprise. "You, Craig Emlyn, don't have that kind of money?" she echoed.

"Well, now, I do and I don't. You see, until I marry, mother and father control all the finances that will someday be mine. Of course, I'll speak to them first thing in the morning and tell them what needs to be done," Craig said comfortingly.

But his words failed to comfort and Millicent felt a terrible uneasiness stirring inside her. "Yes, please do that, darling," she said evenly as they arrived at Haddington Hall.

"Just in case there are some details you might have to fill in, why not come to the house for tea tomorrow," Craig suggested. "Say about four o'clock? We can arrange everything then."

"I shall be there," she said lightly but suddenly she felt as heavy as a lead shot. "Please explain that it's all a matter of putting a quick end to what could be an unnecessary and troublesome problem."

"I shall do that, my dear," Craig said. She let his lips linger for a moment longer than she usually did, then hurried into the house feeling slightly shoddy and thoroughly annoyed with herself. In her room she undressed and pressed her face into the pillow to shut out the world, finally sleeping in semisuffocation until the morning sun woke her. Sarah was finishing muffins and jam when Millicent went downstairs.

"Settle it all last night?" the older woman asked. The question was not put forth maliciously and Millicent was ashamed at her angry retort.

"No, and I'll tell you when I do," she snapped.

"Thank you," Sarah said and Millicent felt as though she could fit comfortably under the table. She tried gardening to keep herself busy during the forenoon, but stopped after clipping three roses off by accident. She was in the carriage early, ordering Rupert to drive very slowly to the Emlyn house. She had no fears of Craig convincing his parents to release the necessary funds to him, she told herself. She just disliked having to explain it all over again to that bloodless couple and having to face Lady Emlyn's unsympathetic manner. When she arrived at the big house, Craig greeted her at the door. His smile was not the usual rakishly sweeping one, she thought, or was she imagining it?

Lord Emlyn was standing in his usual stiff posture beside the tall-backed chair in which Lady Emlyn sat, looking as though she had been carved there. Her smile was as coldly mechanical as always. "Well, now, I presume Craig has told you about the positively irritating problem that has come about." Millicent smiled as she settled herself into a chair opposite the couple. Craig stayed beside her.

"Yes, as much as he could," the woman said. "I must say I don't understand the legal problems if the allegations are preposterous, but then I've never been good at understanding legal matters."

Millicent caught the question encased in the casualness of the remark. Her glance went to Lord Emlyn. "The accusations that have been made are really quite unimportant," Millicent smiled. "It's the legal technicalities they have brought up that are so bothersome."

"I hardly think any accusation is unimportant," Lady Emlyn said. "Accusations must be answered properly and dispensed with once and for all, don't you think?"

"Of course," Millicent said and felt her palms growing damp. "I have answered them, but in this case the situation is such that the matter could be drawn out interminably and I don't want that, especially now with so much to do in regard to the wedding."

"I told mother and father what you said about purchasing Haddington Hall on the open market and putting an end to the entire business," Craig volunteered. Millicent glanced at him, and waited, but he said nothing further. She heard Lord Emlyn's voice, dry as sunbaked wood.

"I'm afraid we've too many houses, now," the man said. "There's this one, of course, the one in Wessex and the cottage in Scotland, plus the chateau on the Riviera. We hardly need another, my dear. It's really quite out of the question."

Millicent forced her smile to stay. "I'm sorry to hear that," she said slowly. Her eyes went to Craig, and saw him shrug apologetically.

"Is it true that the College of Arms has received a set of accusations from Dean Fowler?" Lady Emlyn asked with cold sweetness.

Millicent turned her glance to the woman. "It doesn't take long for news of this sort to be bandied about, does it?" she remarked.

"Some news does travel faster than others," the woman said. "Such accusations within the province

245

of the Keepers of the Blood would, of course, affect a great deal more than legal matters."

"Yes, I suppose they would," Millicent said and suddenly felt quite empty.

"One's social standing would be affected, wouldn't you say?" the woman slid out.

"It could be," Millicent said. She rose, and took the two people in with one quick glance, not hiding the defiance in her eyes. "Thank you for having listened to me," she said, turning to Craig. "Will you see me out, Craig? I do have to be going."

Craig flashed her a quick smile. "Of course," he said, taking her arm, pressing it tightly. Millicent left the room with him, and halted only when they'd reached the door. She looked squarely at him and once again he half-shrugged. "Sorry about the way it turned out," he said. "I did try to make them understand."

"I'm sure you did, Craig," Millicent said. "As much as you're able to make them understand anything."

"I don't understand what that means," he replied with a frown.

"Nothing at all," Millicent answered.

"About announcing the wedding date next month," Craig began. "Mother thinks it might be best to postpone that for now. At least until this whole business clears up a bit."

"And what do you think, Craig?" Millicent asked,

246

watching his face. He half-smiled and looked uncertain.

"I don't know," he answered. "Mother and father both seem to feel that this involves rather serious accusations. They're quite insistent on our waiting."

"And you agree," Millicent said.

Craig looked uncomfortable. "It's not a matter of agreeing. It's just a matter of what's proper."

"I shall tell you what it is," Millicent said. "It's a matter of not being engaged at all now, isn't it?"

"Now I didn't say that, Millicent," he began to protest but she cut him off.

"Not in so many words. By omission, only. Same thing, really. I shall save you further embarrassment. I shall send a notice to the *Times* ending our engagement," Millicent told him.

"No need to rush that," Craig mumbled, looking pained.

"No, no, a day or two will be plenty of time, won't it," Millicent bit out. She gave a harsh little laugh. She didn't even want to slap him. It was simply all finished, only emptiness left. She walked to the carriage and entered without a backward glance. The soft sound of the horse's hooves were strangely soothing. She went into the study when she saw Sarah there and perched herself on the edge of one of the straight-backed chairs. Sarah's eyes studied her for a silent moment, then the woman came to her, put her arms around her, and held her quietly.

"You were afraid this would happen," Millicent said finally.

"I know how quickly news travels and I know where those people attach importance," Sarah said.

Millicent sat back in the chair. "You know, Sarah, I feel strangely detached. I wasn't really surprised at what happened. I suppose I had more than a premonition. I'm not even surprised at Craig, or angry at him, either. I think saddened might be a more appropriate word." She paused, a wry little smile sliding across her lovely lips. "That is hardly the reaction of a woman in love, is it?" she said.

"Hardly," Sarah smiled.

"But then you were right about that all along, weren't you, dear, wise Sarah," Millicent finished ruefully. She rose to her feet. "I think I'll go up to my room. I'd rather like to be alone," she said.

Sarah nodded and Millicent mounted the stairs, then folded herself into a chair by the window and watched the night come. She stayed alone in the dark room, the night a protection. No prying eyes could watch through the blackness, no eager tongues could be heard discussing her. It was over; the bold venture had failed. It had begun so promisingly and come to nothing, every dream shattered, every hope turned to ashes. Only yesterday she would have denied the possibility of what she faced today.

She felt a short, wry gasp leave her lips. Perhaps the bold venture had been doomed to fail. The right thing for the wrong reasons, truth striking back, refusing to be used in so cavalier a manner. She had planned to seek love but it had been the wrong way to find love, wrong from its very inception. Love found by deceit could only be a deception. Perhaps she had deserved Dean's deceit.

His face appeared before her and at once she felt bitterness well up inside her. Sarah had been right all along. Craig had been just a way of striking back at Dean, a refuge for her own hurt. A small laugh of bitterness escaped her lips. The monarchy could have a regent king but the heart refused a regent love. Craig had never been more than that, a substitute. Dean didn't know how he had actually done her a tremendous service. He had rescued her from a life of deceit, a marriage that would have ended in emotional death.

When the great house was absolutely still, Millicent rose and went downstairs. In the study, she traced her fingers along the smooth, rich paneling. She lighted a lamp, and followed its glow into the grand drawing room, the glowing foyer. It was as though she had lived a lifetime here; leaving the house would be the most heartrending of all. In making it come alive again, in restoring all its magnificence, she had come to be one with it, to love every inch of its beauty. In some unknown manner, its great heritage had reached itself around her. She'd felt pride at having given it a renewed glory and had felt warm and sheltered here. She and Haddington Hall had exchanged gifts of the spirit as well as of the body. Slowly, Millicent returned to her room, and when she finally slept, her cheeks were wet with silent tears.

Millicent hardly left the house during the following days. There was no reason for her to do so but, more importantly, she wanted to spend as much time as she could before the time of parting came. "No illusions about that, is there?" she said to Sarah. "The exchequer will signal the end if nothing else does."

"We've another month or so worth of funds. We could give a last party, send invitations to everyone, and see who comes," Sarah said.

"Oh, that would be delicious," Millicent said, warming to the thought. "What's your guess about how many would come?"

"I doubt that any would appear," Sarah said truthfully.

But that very afternoon there was an unexpected visitor. In astonishment, Millicent greeted the Countess de Berrie as her carriage drew up before the door.

"You'll forgive the impoliteness of coming unannounced, but I was passing nearby," the Countess said.

"Please sit down," Millicent responded after recovering from her shock.

"I can't stay but a few minutes. I just wanted to tell you that I am sorry it has all come to this unhappy end. But, if it's of any consolation, you are still the talk of every gathering, every social event of any size. I daresay you will be for the remainder of the season."

"A negative honor, I'm afraid," Millicent said.

"I do like you, my dear, and I wish there was something I could do to help, but I'm afraid that's impossible," the woman said.

"Is it? With your position, I imagine that if you invited me to one of your gatherings, the others would fall in line," Millicent said. "The august gentlemen of the College of Arms might even hear of it and be influenced."

"But that's out of the question, my dear, I couldn't do that. You see, you violated the rules of the game, perhaps the basic rule. It's quite all right to castigate us, to heap ridicule upon us while being a part of the scene. It's perfectly all right to be supremely bitchy, to twist the truth, to cheat and lie. It's all part of the game. But it's not all right to make fools of us and that's what you did, my dear. That, I'm afraid, is unforgiveable." The Countess rose, and extended her hand to Millicent. "Take care of yourself, my dear. I do hope we can lunch sometime, just you and I."

"On another level," Millicent said.

"Of course, on another level," the Countess said. Sarah ushered her to the door, returned, and Millicent shook her head slowly.

"I think I understood what she was trying to say," Millicent remarked. "Though I'm not quite certain."

"You'll have plenty of time to think about it, not that it's worth too much time," Sarah answered.

The very next morning a letter came from Robert Ackrood, the careful, precise script now quite familiar to Millicent. She heaved a deep sigh as she read the brief epistle. She had no emotions left for more than that.

My Dear Madam Hardesty,

Having received no reply or refutation from you which in any way counters the statements made by Mr. Fowler, I must inform you that I have been forced to accept his offer for Haddington Hall, and in so doing I abide by the last letter to him written by Sir Thomas.

As of the twelfth of this month, the title to Haddington Hall shall pass over to Mr. Fowler.

Respectfully,
Robert Ackrood, Esquire

"Not even a *regretfully,*" Millicent commented as she handed the letter to Sarah.

"The twelfth. That's Saturday," Sarah said. "We'd best start packing."

"That won't take terribly long," Millicent said ruefully. "My personal belongings, that's all. Everything else belongs here." She went to Sarah, and put her arms around the wide form. "I'm sorry I talked you into this wild scheme," she said. "But we almost made it come true."

"I enjoyed every minute of it," Sarah said. "And I am back in England."

"Four days left here," Millicent said sadly.

"We'll have a regal dinner every night, just for the two of us," Sarah said. "We may as well go out in high style."

"Why not?" Millicent agreed. "Why not."

The few days left were spent in packing, the hours suddenly terribly precious, and Millicent couldn't decide whether she was emptier inside or out. Sarah kept her promise of the small, elegant dinners and the servants were told they could stay on with their two weeks pay to see if the new owner of Haddington Hall wanted to retain them. The severance pay all but depleted the exchequer and it seemed entirely appropriate to finish the last bottle of *Chateau Lafitte* at dinner.

It was Friday afternoon when Millicent, carrying a vase of flowers to the library, heard the sound of a horse galloping to a halt outside. She opened the door to see a gray stallion wheeling in a half-circle, and fury exploded inside her. Dean looked down at her, his face unsmiling, handsome imperiousness in his eyes. It seemed almost a repetition of their very first meeting. She stepped outside, her cheeks growing hot, and was surprised at the rage that consumed her, obliterating the emptiness she had felt for days.

"Have you come to gloat?" she bit out. "Or just

to see if I'm packed?" He didn't answer and she felt her voice rising. "You are on my property, sir. I order you to leave it this instant. Your title doesn't take effect until tomorrow," she flung at him.

He reached inside his white silk shirt, and pulled forth a piece of rolled parchment, which he tossed at her feet as the stallion reared up on its hind legs. "It won't take effect then, either," he snapped, then wheeled the horse around and raced away. Millicent stared after him, a sob breaking inside her throat. A last strange, cryptic remark, she murmured. He couldn't let her go without one last such remark. She bent down, aware that Sarah had come to the doorway, and picked up the rolled parchment. She opened it, her eyes widening.

"It's the deed to Haddington Hall," she gasped. "And it's been signed over to me." She turned, staring at Sarah, then whirled, and ran to the stables. She flung a bit and bridle over one of the horses, added a blanket in place of a saddle, and climbed onto the animal. She was almost in a full gallop as she raced from the stable. The distance to Dean's estate seemed an eternity, yet it was hardly more than a quarter mile. Was he engaging in some kind of cruelty? What did it mean? The questions whirled around inside her and she knew she had to have answers. The gray stallion was standing at the hitching post alongside the house and she halted beside the horse, tied her mount, and started for the front door.

Dean emerged, his face still unsmiling, and halted

before her. "What does this mean?" she asked, holding up the roll in her hand. "I don't understand," she said honestly.

"It means Haddington Hall is yours," he answered curtly. She took another step closer to him, her heart pounding wildly. She didn't dare to grasp the thought that speared at her. It was too much to hope and yet there was nothing else to think.

"Why?" she asked, tearing the single word from her throat. "Why, after all you've said, all you've done to win?"

"It was the only way left to me," he said. "You refused to listen, to let me explain. But I had to have Haddington Hall first."

"And the wager?" Millicent asked, her voice suddenly as small as she felt.

"It was made when I first met you, before I fell in love with you. I never gave it another thought," Dean said. "But I saw that you'd never have believed me. If I'd told you I wanted Haddington Hall for you, would you have listened, believed me then?"

"No, probably not," Millicent admitted. "And Cynthia, what of her?"

"Cynthia was an involvement of resentment, not of love," Dean said with a half smile. "And she knew as much."

His arms reached out suddenly, grasped her, and pulled her to him. "Now you've no choice left but to believe. Haddington Hall is yours," he said savagely. His mouth found hers, pressing down hungrily.

"Dean, Dean my love," she said between kisses. "I've been so wrong about everything. I know that now."

"I had to have Haddington Hall to give you before your wedding plans went too far," he said. "I knew it was the one thing that would make you believe in me."

"The wedding plans," she echoed, not so much with regret as with relief. "They ended before this, my darling."

He drew back, and looked at her. His eyes held a small, secret smile. "The one thing that I held tight to was knowing how much you loved me," he said.

She frowned at once. "You are still the most arrogant man. Why would you have known any such thing?" she returned.

"Anyone who hated so much had to love just as much," he said softly. She buried her face in his chest. He wasn't the most arrogant man after all, she murmured silently. He was the most wise. She'd have to tell Sarah that, she promised herself as a meadowlark began to sing. Pure, clear, sweet, its song was nevertheless nothing compared with the song in her heart.